The trouble with
Donovan
Croft

Bernard Ashley

The trouble with Donovan Croft

OXFORD
UNIVERSITY PRESS

OXFORD
UNIVERSITY PRESS

Great Clarendon Street, Oxford OX2 6DP

Oxford University Press is a department of the University of Oxford.
It furthers the University's objective of excellence in research, scholarship,
and education by publishing worldwide in

Oxford   New York

Auckland   Cape Town   Dar es Salaam   Hong Kong   Karachi
Kuala Lumpur   Madrid   Melbourne   Mexico City   Nairobi
New Delhi   Shanghai   Taipei   Toronto

With offices in

Argentina   Austria   Brazil   Chile   Czech Republic   France   Greece
Guatemala   Hungary   Italy   Japan   Poland   Portugal   Singapore
South Korea   Switzerland   Thailand   Turkey   Ukraine   Vietnam

Oxford is a registered trade mark of Oxford University Press
in the UK and in certain other countries

British Library Cataloguing in Publication Data available

ISBN: 978-0-19-275556-8

3 5 7 9 10 8 6 4 2

Printed in Great Britain

Paper used in the production of this book is a natural,
recyclable product made from wood grown in sustainable forests.
The manufacturing process conforms to the environmental
regulations of the country of origin.

BEFORE YOU START

Have you ever been pushed around by a teacher? Or verbally abused? Has racist language been used towards you and nothing done about it by the school's adults? Do you think a headteacher would organize their pupils in a search of the district for a missing boy — and in school time? It's all very unlikely, yet these sorts of things could have happened in the 1970s when *The Trouble with Donovan Croft* was first published in Britain, when society was so much less aware of racism and sexism, of Health and Safety — and when the cane was still swishing in many schools.

It was a different society then in many ways. Street language changes all the time, popular music changes, attitudes and fashion change —but the seventies were especially distinctive in the looks and the sounds around. Hit songs were recorded onto '45s' and 'LPs' by 'pop singers' not 'bands', and played on living room 'music centres' instead of iPods and MP3s. And some of the elderly musicians who are honoured today were smashing their instruments on stage and trashing hotel rooms. Long hair was the fashion for boys, with thick soled shoes, tank tops, and bomber jackets. Holidays were still mainly with parents (and there were more families with both mothers and fathers), while schools were different from today. There was no national curriculum, and only a few local authorities were beginning to be aware of the educational needs of newcomers to Britain. Primary school uniform was less common, 'Year Six' was called 'Fourth Year Junior' (which I have modernized in this edition for clarity), and no parent or visitor had to seek entry to the school, or wear a badge when they got inside. There was no satellite TV, just two terrestrial channels (on which you never heard the 'f' word) and there were no laptops, eBooks, iPaqs or computer games, while even photocopiers were still in the prototype stage — and a pocket calculator cost sixty pounds in seventies money. Football hooliganism was a weekly event at grounds all over the country — where most spectators stood instead of having obligatory seats — and race and anti-nuclear marches were common. In the popular High Street bookshops in the East End of London very few books had black central characters, with little in fiction to reflect the lives of the Asian, Greek, and Caribbean families who passed their doors. Indeed, *The Trouble with Donovan Croft* was one of the few books to be published with a black hero; while it was also one of the early school stories to be set in a state and not a public school.

In those days comparatively little was known about 'elective mutism' — from which Donovan suffers in the book – although my research did show that the largest single group of sufferers were newly arrived black male teenagers, which is why I made Donovan who he is.

The book is of its period, but I hope the story is still pacy and exciting — and it contains what hasn't changed, the crucial relationship that can exist between one person and another; in this case the 'brother' love that grows between two boys.

BERNARD ASHLEY
2008

1

Keith Chapman, a tall, fair boy in blue jeans and a T-shirt, held his breath and hurried past number fifty-one, 'the dirty house'. He hated passing the place and he always did so at top speed. With grimy windows and peeling paintwork, sitting in the middle of the terrace like a decaying tooth in a good set, it was a place to be avoided. The house was said to be owned by an old woman with a hole in her forehead, and none of Keith's friends paused outside for long. As usual, Keith released his breath after a count of twenty (a known precaution against evil) and ran round the last corner to the school. He paused before he crossed the road and looked up at the big building with unenthusiastic eyes. It seemed all wrong to be coming to school today, even for ten minutes on the last day of the holidays. Holidays were holidays and school was school, Keith thought. Not that anyone in the area could forget the existence of the school for long.

Transport Avenue Junior School rose above the surrounding streets like a cathedral in a medieval town, tall, aloof, and built to stand forever. Its red brick turrets had dwarfed the terraces of City East for nearly a hundred years. Its bell had called children through its separate gates, its GIRLS, its BOYS, and its BABIES for generations. And still the children came; although no one rang the turret bell any more, and the teachers now had different ways of segregating them.

1

Once again, on the day before an autumn term started, the school had that odd look of being ready and waiting. The playground had been swept clean of sweet papers. Some of the broken windows had been mended, and the rest had been patched up with fresh-looking cardboard. There were new white netball markings on the ground and two new dustbins shone at the top of the cellar steps.

Keith looked at the peaceful scene. Then he walked across the playground as if it were a minefield. During the holidays this was enemy territory, guarded against invaders by Mr Harper the caretaker. Even the teachers' children usually crossed it as quickly as possible or played very quiet games well away from the cellar steps while their parents were busy in school. It wasn't that Mr Harper had two heads or a forked tail. In fact, his slight figure in an over-large boiler-suit gave him more the air of a drowned rat. He just thought that schools and playgrounds were nicer, quieter places to work in when there were no children about.

Although Keith was on official business, he would sooner not have to explain it to a shouting Mr Harper from the cellar. So he ran lightly on his Tuf shoes across the smooth tarmac. Longish fair hair, always tangled and curling at the ends when he got hot, fell down over his brown eyes as he ran head-down for the door marked GIRLS. He need not have worried. Mr Harper was too busy at his bench putting back the parts of his starter motor (and getting one part left over every time) to bother about a nervous boy.

Inside the tall Victorian building the butterflies in Keith's stomach fluttered more furiously. The walls stripped of last term's work, the floors gleaming with new Seal, the classrooms locked against tipsy wedding guests on Saturdays—it all seemed unfamiliar and unfriendly. Without Dave, Tony, and the rest, the place didn't seem like his school at all. And without Miss Davis, Keith thought, it would all be worse tomorrow. It was always worse, the bigger boys said, in Mr Henry's class.

Keith walked round the edge of the hall and up the stairs at the end to the headmaster's room. Through the crinkly glass, Keith could see the large shape of Mr Roper behind his desk. He seemed to be standing very still, head up, as he did in assembly when he waited for a late class to come in, or for 'Trumpet Voluntary' (his favourite record) to finish. Keith knocked.

'Come!' boomed Mr Roper, like someone important in a television play; then he thought better of it, coughed, and called again. 'Come in.'

Keith went in and shut the door behind him. The sun shone in through the half-netted window and cast a dusty spotlight on Mr Roper's high-domed bald head. With his horn-rimmed glasses and benign smile he always resembled a mad scientist, jovial yet sinister; and today his holiday outfit of clinically white linen jacket and flannels did little to destroy the effect.

'Good morning, Keith,' he said, sitting down and covering a letter on his desk with a notebook. 'You're wanting to make an early start.' He laughed gently and raised his eyebrows as if to ask what Keith really wanted. But Keith, not being one of the teachers, didn't catch this meaning and just answered:

'Morning, Mr Roper.'

'And what can I do for you?'

Keith handed over his mother's note. Mr Roper unfolded the sheet of writing-paper and read the small handwriting which sat neatly on the lines.

'23 Lennox Road,
City East.
9th September.

'Dear Sir,

The Welfare Dept. have asked my husband and me to foster a boy from a Jamaican family for a few months. As he is the same age as Keith, would it be possible for him to be with Keith in class? His name is Donovan Croft. I can give you his other details tomorrow. His reports will be sent on from his other school later. I will bring him up in the morning if you can take him.

Yours truly,

Doreen Chapman (Mrs)'

Mr Roper put the letter in a wire tray on his desk. This was nothing new. Children came and went at Transport Avenue with very little ceremony. He ran over the new classes in his head.

'Yes, tell Mother that's all right. I don't think Mr Henry's class is over-full this term. Bring the boy with you. And if Mother comes at nine-thirty, after assembly, I'll be able to see her then.'

'Yes, sir.'

'Off you go, then, and mind the hall floor. I think it's still wet in some places.'

'Yes, sir.'

Keith went back down the stairs and made a great display of walking carefully round the edge of the Sealed floor, while Mr Roper watched him from the top of the steps, like a ship's captain on the bridge. Mr Roper remembered the time when the Chairman of Managers had walked right across the hall floor one half-term about an hour after the caretaker had put wet Seal on it.

'Such a hot day,' the Chairman had said, 'and quite sticky underfoot.'

The caretaker hadn't laughed when Mr Roper went down to the cellar to tell him.

The caretaker wasn't laughing now. His starter still wouldn't go back together, and the last thing he wanted was to have to go back to the garage and buy the new one they said he needed. He went up the cellar steps to rattle a dustbin and sound busy to the cleaners. Then he saw Keith coming through the door.

'Hey, you, what are you doing here?' he asked, emerging like a policeman from the cells. 'I don't want you in here till the morning. I've got Seal on that hall floor.'

'I know,' said Keith. 'Mr Roper told me. I had to see Mr Roper for my mum.'

'Oh well, that's all right, then. Now off with you quick.'

Then, without a further glance, Mr Harper disappeared into the cellar to do battle with the starter once more.

Keith ran out through the gate, then walked home. He walked slowly, unaware of the busy streets around him, thinking. His thoughts were a bit muddled, but they all boiled down to his being worried about the next day or so. Back to school after the summer holidays always gave him mixed feelings: swapping the freedom of playing round the streets with his mates for the routine of school never seemed so good at first, but then he'd always enjoyed school once he got there. This year, though, it was different; it wasn't just another start in a new class, but a first start with a man teacher. Not that he would have minded going into Mr Bryan's class, the bearded teacher who took boys' games and played a guitar in singing. No, that would have been all right. He would have got on quite well with Mr Bryan. But Mr Henry was another matter. He was short, fat, and old (at least forty-five) with a loud, shouting voice which always took the mickey out of you. Keith had fallen foul of him one playtime, when his ball had hit Mr Henry on the back of the leg.

'Come here, lad,' the teacher had shouted. 'A bit careless, aren't we?' He gave the word 'careless' a short staccato bite. 'Give it here. And don't do it again.' Since he never gave the ball back he made sure the odds were on Keith obeying the last instruction. The bigger boys said he could be a lot like that in class. He kept everyone sitting in rows, there was no moving about, and the only jokes were those he cracked about the kids. He talked a lot about things they didn't understand and he was a bit handy with his ruler. No, Keith wasn't looking forward to a year with Mr Henry.

The other thing worrying Keith was this Donovan coming to live at their house for a few months. Keith's brother, Alan, was married now and Keith had been on his own with his mum and dad for a year or so. It was going to be different, having another boy about. There was a spare room for him to sleep in, but Keith would still have a lot of sharing to do. The Chapmans had had a boy to live with them when Keith was small, and by the time he had left, he had broken just about all the toys Keith had. There hadn't been any foster-children since, and Keith had forgotten all about it. Till now. It struck him suddenly today. In a few hours now Donovan would arrive and Keith would be a foster-brother once more. Foster-brother. The title sounded too strong to describe a bond formed so suddenly.

It came out of the blue, the letter to Keith's parents asking them to consider fostering again. It explained itself as being part of a general scheme to find more homes for children in need.

'They must've gone through their old lists,' Mrs Chapman said when she discussed it with her husband.

'But I'm not sure, Ted, not about doing it again. It wouldn't be fair on Keith . . .'

That was their main concern, the effect it would have on their own son. If there was any chance of it harming him they would rather not take the risk. Keith heard them say so. They left it like that for a couple of weeks, and it seemed to have been forgotten, until one night when the BBC transmitted a programme from a large children's home. The sight of so many motherless children, 'those sad, innocent eyes' Mrs Chapman called them, brought up the whole business again, and they talked the matter over into the small hours of the morning. Keith, they finally decided, was really very lucky, and there were a lot of children in the world who were not. They would send the letter back the next morning agreeing to foster again.

Neither of them slept very well that night, and when the letter was posted next morning, they each had unspoken doubts about the wisdom of their action. When they told Keith about their decision he said very little. He was engrossed in a comic and he hardly seemed to hear. Mrs Chapman said as much to her husband.

'Of course he heard,' he said. 'But kids don't make any bones about this sort of thing. They take it in their stride. Still, you were right to tell him . . .'

Mrs Chapman thought for a moment. 'Yes,' she said. 'I was. But all the same I wish I'd asked instead . . .'

For Keith, though, it had been a decision of his parents and that was that. It'd probably work out. No good worrying too much. But it would be strange actually having a boy living indoors. He got on well with most of the black kids at school, but having one at home all the time would be bound to be a bit different.

Keith's mother must have felt the same because she couldn't quite settle to anything while Keith was taking the message to school until she had explained it all to Mrs

Parsons next door. She didn't want the boy to arrive in the car without the ground being prepared. Mrs Parsons could be quite put out over some things.

Keith let himself in through the front door just as his mother got to the crux of things over a low part of the fence at the back. Mrs Parsons, a short, thin woman, just too old in Mr Chapman's opinion for the mini-skirts she wore, was pegging out an apricot coloured nightie and one sock.

'Yes, he's a dear little boy from a West Indian family,' said Mrs Chapman.

'Oh,' said Mrs Parsons, a bit straight. 'I know there's a lot about,' as if she were talking about an illness. 'Why's he coming all this way to you?'

Mrs Chapman realized that she had given the wrong impression about Donovan.

'Well, he's not coming so far,' she replied, 'only from North London. His father works there in a factory. Now his mother has been called back to nurse her father in Jamaica, and the authorities say Donovan's father can't look after him properly on his own. He works such long hours. So Donovan's being fostered by us until his mother comes back.'

'Oh, I see,' said Mrs Parsons. 'Very nice for them too, I suppose. Just up and leave the children and we have to pay out to have them looked after.' She made it sound as if Mrs Chapman were making a gigantic profit out of some personal welfare service provided by Mr and Mrs Parsons. She began to stuff some spare pegs into her skirt pocket, ready to go indoors.

'It's not quite as bad as it seems,' Mrs Chapman put in quickly. 'The father's paying for his keep. But even if he wasn't, they've lived here for twelve years, and Donovan was born here. So really he's as British as you and I.'

Mrs Parsons looked offended.

'Besides, his parents pay rates and taxes just like us, so they're entitled to some of the benefits when they need them. And I'm sure you wouldn't like to see a little boy left to roam the streets in all weathers till his dad comes home at eight o'clock. You wouldn't have liked that for your Ronnie.'

She drew a breath, surprised at her own flow of words.

'Yes, well that's true, I suppose,' said Mrs Parsons, definitely going in now. 'But things have changed a lot since I moved in here.' She bent awkwardly to pick up a fallen peg on the way. 'And not all for the better.'

Mrs Chapman sighed and turned away. Mrs Parsons had taken the news much as she had feared, and things weren't going to be all sweetness and light between the neighbours for the next few months, that was clear. However, she was not the sort of person to be put off a thing by somebody's stupid attitude. She hurried into the house. There were things to be done. A dinner to cook, a bed to make up, and a room to prepare for Donovan.

'Come on, give us a hand,' she said as she saw Keith back from the school and sitting in a chair. 'Did you see Mr Roper? Is everything all right?'

'Yes,' said Keith. 'It's all OK. He said you've got to go up at half past nine in the morning.'

'Good, well let's get ready for him. You can tidy out your toy cupboard to start with.'

She hurried out of the room and up the stairs to prepare a welcome for Donovan, who would probably arrive feeling very strange and none too happy. Meanwhile, Keith pulled himself slowly out of the chair and stuck his hands in his pockets. More work! He didn't exactly look a picture of happiness himself.

2

When Keith tidied anything, the saying 'things will get worse before they get better' always held true. Except when people were coming, his bedroom had a very lived-in look, rather like the scene of a burglary in a television play. Now he had to sort out his toy cupboard, at least enough to shut the door, so its contents were spread all over the floor and the bed. 'Action Man', minus a foot and with a string round his neck where the enemy had hanged him after capture, lay slumped against an empty fish-tank. Bits of Lego and Meccano were mixed up with cars and bright bending strips of Hot Wheel track. An army of khaki troops lay sloping arms in death amongst assorted cowboys, indians, and knights in armour, and felt pens, peeling wooden bricks, and pieces of various jigsaws were scattered everywhere.

Keith lay amongst them on the floor reading last year's 'Score' annual. Every tidy-up revealed some forgotten treasure. This had been lost so long that Keith looked through it again as if it were new. It seemed quite dated, though, although it was only last year's: several top players were pictured playing for clubs they had left, and all the haircuts seemed old-fashioned. The City East team was represented by only one photograph: a black-and-white action picture where the ball appeared to be a player's head. 'BALLING THE HEAD' was the caption. But since City was a Third Division side with no star players, this scant interest was only to be expected. Keith flicked through to the end of the book. It would be great if

Donovan liked football. The thought cheered him up. They could sometimes go and see City play. They could swap football cards and share 'Scores'. They could go round the park, or have a Subbuteo league. If Donovan liked football.

'Keith! Have you finished?' Mrs Chapman called from beneath a pile of bedding. 'Is everything back in that cupboard yet?'

'Yes, almost.' Keith bent the truth towards him.

'Well, hurry up and get done and you can help me put the finishing touches to Donovan's room.'

Donovan's room. That sounded odd. Up to now it had been Alan's room, or, since his marriage, the spare room. Alan and his wife squeezed into the single bed on their rare overnight visits, otherwise it was part of Keith's territory, where he sometimes got out his trains or anything else he wanted to leave out for a few days. But now it was Donovan's room. Where Donovan could shut the door and keep him out if he wanted. That would take some getting used to. Keith tried his own door to see if it would shut. Yes, it did. He had never bothered before, that was all.

He compressed his toys, unsorted, into three cardboard cartons and stuffed them in the cupboard, but his thoughts were miles away, his head filled with questions about the other boy.

Would Donovan want different programmes on the telly? Would he spoil Keith's gang with Dave and Tony? Would he have to go everywhere with Keith, all the time?

'Keith,' called Mrs Chapman, still in Donovan's room. 'Finish that and find me a bulb for this table-lamp, will you? He can have a light by his bed then.'

Keith went down and looked in the cupboard under the stairs, in the biscuit-tin where his dad sometimes kept spares. But the only bulb in there was a red one left over from Christmas. Keith went back to his room, took the bulb from a light clipped on to his headboard and went into the spare room with it.

Just now Mrs Chapman was busy giving it a bit of character, making it look a bit more than just the spare room with the bed made up. She pinned to the wall a map of lifeboat stations in the British Isles (printed on a tea-towel they had bought at Clacton) and she stood six Grand Prix table-mats ready to race along the mantelpiece.

'It's not much, but it's a start,' she said to Keith. 'You can help him to make it more like home later.'

Keith handed her the bulb.

'Good boy. Where was this?'

Keith stuck his hands in his pockets. 'It was spare,' he said.

They waited a long time for Donovan to arrive. Looking out through the front-room window, Keith saw the last day of the summer holiday slip away. It was always strange and quiet in there, not really part of the house, a bit spooky. You could almost hear the silence, the tick of the clock and the odd creak of under-used furniture. It was no place to be when the sun was shining and school was shut.

Tony and Dave knocked for him soon after dinner.

'Coming out, Kee?'

'No, I can't.'

'You promised.'

'I forgot about today.'

'We're going up the flat lifts.'

'I can't.'

'Why?'

'This kid's coming to stay. I've got to wait for him.'

'Oh. Well, please yourself then.'

13

'See you tomorrow.'

'Yeah, s'pose so.'

Tony and Dave walked away together. Outside the gate, Dave said something and Tony doubled up laughing. Keith didn't know what the joke was, but it sounded like one of Dave's famous rude remarks. A funny sort of pain, as real as bellyache, passed across Keith's middle. It lasted for about five minutes, then it disappeared as the sound of Dave's laughter faded from his ears.

While Keith sat staring out of the window, Mrs Chapman busied herself about the house. She was one of those people who cannot relax. She was never finished. Her husband often complained about her constant activity, partly because he wanted her to rest, and partly because she made him feel bad sitting watching the television. And when she did sit down she was knitting or sewing. This afternoon, when everything was prepared, she went round the house with a warm cloth wiping all the door handles and finger plates—which were all perfectly clean before she started.

The September sun, losing its summer heat early, had felled the plane-trees in black shadows across the road before Donovan's car drove up. At first Keith took no notice of the arrival; he was looking for a big black limousine; but when a small grey Morris 1000 stopped dead outside the window, he jumped off the settee and ran to shout down the hall:

'They're here. The car's here.' Then he went back to the settee and knelt up away from the net curtains so as not to be seen. Mrs Chapman opened the front door and walked the three metres to the gate.

From out of the driver's door of the Morris emerged a tanned middle-aged woman wearing thick tortoise-shell glasses and a bright blue blazer and skirt. Her lips were almost fluorescently bright, and so was her smile. In her hand, instead of the fat briefcase Mrs Chapman had expected to see, she carried a small square handbag which looked most unofficial. With a wave she walked round the front of the car and up to the gate.

'Hallo, dear,' she said. 'Here we are, safe and sound and sorry to be late. Everything was going to plan until Donovan decided he didn't want to come and there was a bit of a to-do. I think he thought we were taking him off to prison.' She laughed loudly.

'Oh, but didn't you explain?' asked Mrs Chapman.

'Of course, dear, of course,' the woman replied in her fast, lilting voice. 'But he wasn't listening, was he? He didn't take it in. So anyway his dad and I got him in the car, and here he is. Give him his tea and a bit of love and he'll be fine.'

She threw her last words over her shoulder as she walked to the rear of the car. She opened the boot one-handed and swung out a small grey suitcase. This she carried through into the Chapmans' hall.

'Here you are, dear, one suitcase, not much clothing, but we'll see you OK for buying more. Oh, and no pyjamas. He'll need a pair of those.'

Mrs Chapman was about to ask if he had been allowed to bring any favourite toys, when she realized she hadn't even seen the boy yet. She peered over the welfare officer's shoulder. But she couldn't see anyone. As far as she could see the car was empty.

Donovan was there, though. Keith had seen him. From his perch in the front room he had only had eyes for the back seat of the car. At first sight it certainly seemed to be empty. As he looked harder, though, he saw a movement in the far corner, the turn of a dark head of tightly curled black hair, slumped down on a grey anorak. Then there was a total stillness—head down, mouth shut in a downward curve, eyes open but not looking—a far cry from the bright-eyed face at the car window which Keith and his mother had each imagined.

The welfare officer walked over to the car, opened the driver's door and tipped the seat forward.

'Come on, old son, we're here. Out you get, one, two, three.'

But there was no response. Donovan stayed where he was, sitting back in the seat, his hands in his coat pockets. His feet just missed the floor and his legs hung unmoving.

'Come on, old sunshine, come and meet Mrs Chapman. She's got everything ready for you.'

Donovan neither moved nor answered. The welfare officer drummed her fingers on the bonnet for a few seconds. Then she stood up and looked over the top of the car at Mrs Chapman.

'Won't be a minute,' she called, smiling. 'Just a slight reluctance.' She bent back inside to Donovan. 'Come along. You'll like it here. There's a room of your own and a boy your age to play with. And it's not for ever, is it? Come on, don't be stroppy, sunshine. Out you come. You can't stay in the car all night.'

She might have been talking to a corpse. There was not the slightest twitch, the slightest hint of movement to suggest that Donovan had heard. There were no sullen sighs, no tears, no sobs in the throat. He just sat in the car as still and as silent as a rabbit waiting for a fox to make a move.

'Come on, Donovan,' the welfare officer tried again. 'You're being very silly and you're keeping everyone waiting. What's Mrs Chapman going to think of you if you're awkward?'

She reached a blazered arm into the car towards Donovan's shoulder, careful not to touch him. He didn't pull away, he didn't really move, but the woman was

16

aware of a strong invisible wall between them. She uncoiled from within the car again to find Mrs Chapman standing by her.

'Let me have a go,' she said.

'Well, you can have a try, dear,' said the welfare officer, 'but you'll be lucky to shift him with words in this mood.'

They both stood pressed against the side of the Morris as an old Vauxhall Victor came roaring past a bit too close. Then Mrs Chapman put her head into the car and spoke to Donovan in a soft but cheerful voice.

'Hallo, Donovan; my name's Mrs Chapman. You're coming to stay with me for a little while, until your mother comes back from Jamaica. Everything is going to be all right.'

She stopped to think what to say next. There was no move from Donovan.

'We've got everything ready for you: your own room, a nice bed with a table-lamp, and I've got a boy called Keith for you to play with.'

Keith sounded like a toy. She paused again. Still no move.

'Now, you come with me and we'll have some tea.'

Donovan clearly was not hungry. She smiled at him hopefully. But their eyes did not meet, and there was no sign to show that he had even heard what she had said.

'I'll tell you what, you can choose what you want for tea. Egg and bacon? Beefburgers and chips? Baked beans on toast? You tell me what you like and we'll have it for tea.'

A long silence hung in the air while Mrs Chapman felt a growing sense of defeat. Eventually she stood up out of the car.

'What are we to do?' she asked the welfare officer. 'How did you get him into the car?'

'Oh, his father did that; he just carried him in while I held the door open.'

'Oh.'

Suddenly the welfare officer brightened. 'What time does your husband come home from work, Mrs Chapman? A man is always useful at times like this . . . '

'He gets in in about an hour,' Mrs Chapman replied. 'But I really don't think forcing him is going to do any good. You know, if he won't even get out of the car on his own I wonder if we'll be able to cope with him here. I didn't know he was a problem child.'

'Well, dear, any child without a mother at home has problems, to a greater or lesser degree. But our records show this chap to be quite normal; no one's told me anything about him being particularly awkward.'

The two women looked at one another, baffled. Had Donovan been the son of either of them he would have been out of that car in a flash, upset or not, and they would have thought little more about it. Somebody else's child was another matter, though, and they didn't know quite what to do.

Their predicament was being observed. A movement on the edge of Mrs Chapman's circle of vision caught her attention. It was one of Mrs Parsons' upstairs net curtains moving ever so slightly as the neighbour tried to get a better view through the nylon pattern. Mrs Chapman sighed. So she was watching, was she? Trust her to be seeing all this. Trust her to see Donovan being awkward.

The two women in the street stared at the car, each trying to think of a way to let Donovan out. They both realized it would probably require force, and while the welfare officer was used to 'being firm to be kind', Mrs Chapman was unhappy about manhandling Donovan out of the car. There was a long, long wait while the women thought, and behind them Mrs Parsons moved her curtain clear aside to get a better view.

They were just about to admit defeat when Keith came out of the front door. He had watched his mother and the other lady trying to get Donovan out of the car, and he couldn't just sit and watch the deadlock any longer. Nor could he just wander off to play. Kids understand other kids, he thought. He might be able to do it where his mum couldn't. He walked round to the front of the car with something held behind his back, as if he were playing a game. He didn't want to say anything to his mother, or either of the women to say anything to him, because that would only put him on their side against the boy in the car. And he wanted Donovan to see he was up for him. Luckily both women sensed his feelings from the deliberate way he walked to the car door, and neither of them spoke.

'Hallo, Don,' he said. 'I'm Keith.'

He squeezed in past the tipped-up seat and Donovan's knees and sat next to the silent boy.

'I live here. You're in my class at school. Mr Henry's.'

He stopped for a few seconds. He had produced no reaction in the other.

'Want a hold of this?'

From behind his back he brought the smallest untidiest scrap of white fur imaginable. It looked like something which might be found hanging from a barbed-wire fence or a gorsebush. But it had two pink eyes and two tiny curled-up black ears.

'It's a baby guinea-pig. My dad brought it home last week from the market near his works. It's called Fluff. It doesn't bite.'

He offered Donovan the sniffing scrap of fur on his flattened palm. He could see it was in Donovan's line of vision. But Donovan did not move. Keith held it there until his arm began to ache. Then slowly he put the white bundle down into Donovan's lap.

It is easy to ignore what is heard, or even what is seen; but it is virtually impossible, Keith knew, to ignore a three-week-old guinea-pig snuffling in your lap. As Fluff investigated the changing texture of Donovan's trousers, and tickled as he did so, Donovan slowly took his hands out of his pockets and cupped the animal in them. Like a naturalist with a new species he lifted Fluff up and looked hard at him. He saw the fur which would later grow in whirls fluffing out in all directions; he saw the twitching nose, and the pink eyes which could surely see little in that muddle of fur. Gently his right thumb moved to stroke down the small smooth spine.

There was another long silence. Mrs Chapman and the welfare officer stood motionless outside the car. Keith sat still and silent next to Donovan, while Donovan gently caressed the guinea-pig with his thumbs. Everything stayed like that for a minute or so. Even Mrs Parsons stared from her window without blinking. Then Keith tipped the front seat forward on his side of the car and opened the passenger door. He got out.

'Bring him in for us, Don; I'll show you his hutch,' he said, and he walked away from the car without looking back—but somehow aware of what was happening behind him like a man being covered with a pistol.

Donovan continued to stroke the guinea-pig. It had settled in his warm hands. He sleeked back the fur and watched it fall into disorder as his thumbs passed on. He felt the warmth of the body and the fast beat of the small heart. Suddenly, holding Fluff firmly in his left hand, he pulled himself out of the door Keith had used and walked across the pavement to the front gate.

'Come on, Don,' said Keith. 'Out the back.' He led the

way into the house and, with his head down, concentrating on the guinea-pig, Donovan followed.

'Well, who'd have thought it?' said the welfare officer. 'I was beginning to think I'd have to take him out to the hostel. Bright boy you've got there, Mrs Chapman.'

The welfare officer closed the episode with loud bangings of her car doors.

'Good luck, my dear, and let us know if there's any more bother. I think he'll settle after a day or so.'

Mrs Chapman said goodbye and followed the boys indoors. She hoped the welfare officer was right. Meanwhile, the least she could do now was get the tea.

3

'Well, blow me,' said Ted Chapman. 'That's about the worst meal I've ever had.'

He was standing two steps down from the living-room doing the washing-up at the kitchen sink. Mrs Chapman stood above him, framed in the doorway, folding a floral table-cloth.

'He didn't say a blessed word, just stared at his plate and picked at his food as if it was poison. What's up with him? Is he ill or something?'

'I don't know, Ted,' said Mrs Chapman, coming down to the drawer by the sink. 'I told you we had this business in the street. Well, it was just like you saw at tea-time. That's more or less how he was in the car. Until Keith got him out with the guinea-pig.' She folded the table-cloth away across the tops of the knives and forks. 'Then they went through together into the garden and put it into the hutch. But it was silence all the way. I don't think anything was said, not by Donovan anyway.'

She told her husband how she had followed them through the house and watched them at the hutch from the kitchen window. Donovan had stroked the small guinea-pig continuously, concentrating his hands on it though his mind seemed far away. Keith had shown him where the food and litter were kept and how the water hopper worked. Then, as soon as he had shown him how the hutch door opened, Donovan had put the guinea-pig in and stood away.

'That was the end of that. He followed Keith upstairs

23

and watched him play cars, but he didn't say anything. Keith did all the talking, you know Keith, but I don't think Donovan was paying any attention. In spite of all that they seemed quite matey, though.'

'But he didn't want to know Keith at tea-time, did he?' said Mr Chapman. 'He didn't lift his eyes off his plate.'

He vigorously brushed the grease off a plate with swift sudsy strokes and splashed his shirt with white froth.

'Blast!' he said. 'Never mind what the telly says, there's too much lather with this stuff.'

He was a tall man with thinning auburn hair and a long, strong face. A rare culture of fine down grew among the freckles on the top of his head and a tougher coppery growth gave a strength to his arms and hands. He was a well-built man, neither fat nor muscular. The men at work rarely argued with Ted, a good foreman who had an inner strength about him which demanded respect. No one pulled his leg at work, or treated him with sarcasm. In fact, Ted's workmates were surprised to hear his wife answering him back at the firm's cricket matches, and they thought Keith sometimes got away with murder.

Ted and Doreen Chapman made a solemn-seeming pair to the outside world. They took life seriously, and they saved and used their money cautiously. They put their home life before anything else, rarely went out, and never needed to borrow sugar, bread, or next door's lawn-mower. They lived a quiet life with hardly a ripple to disturb the pool of contentment. Until Donovan dropped into it with a mighty splash.

'He must be very upset,' said Mrs Chapman. 'He must miss his mother very much, and his dad. I expect he'll come out of his shell in a while.'

Upstairs, Keith went on talking. The silence in Donovan's room as he unpacked his suitcase needed filling with something; so Keith first brought in his small transistor and found Radio One, then he kept up a stream of comments on anything which entered his head. At first it was the tinny music.

'I like this, do you? He's got a funny voice but it's quite good. He doesn't half look weird on telly. He's really a teacher, did you know?'

Donovan might have known, but he didn't show it. Mrs Chapman had put his suitcase on his bed and left him to take out his clothes and find his own homes for them. There wasn't much to unpack. His father had got the clothes together in a hurry without thinking too much about the different things Donovan would be doing. Several things, not ready to hand, he had rushed out and bought. There were two new shirts, some clean pants, some socks, and a new vest. There was a grey jumper and two pairs of trousers—one pair old and one pair smart, new, and flared. But there were no slippers, pyjamas, boots, jeans, T-shirts or anything casual.

Seeming to concentrate very hard on what he was doing, Donovan made half a dozen short journeys between the bed and the chest of drawers, while Keith leaned against the window and carried on the one-sided conversation.

'Have you seen those new football boots in Woolworth's? A kid at school got some last year from London. They cost a bomb. They're in Woolworth's this year, though. Mum's getting me some on Saturday. We do proper football in old Henry's class. You know, down the fields, not the playground.' Keith paused for a few seconds, although he didn't really expect a reply. 'What was your school like? Any good? Ours isn't bad, once you get used to it. Old Roper's all right, a bit moody at times. He's mostly quiet, but sometimes he shouts a lot. Nothing like old Henry, though . . . '

Keith stopped, his flow of words stemmed by the look on Donovan's face. He was staring down with intent eyes and an open mouth. Keith thought he had frightened him with his remarks about Mr Roper and Mr Henry. But that wasn't it. It was something in Donovan's case.

Donovan's father had forgotten a lot of important things when packing the case: but under the vest at the bottom, flat and smooth, lay a glossy photograph of a football team in full colour, and something in Donovan's attitude seemed to show that his father had remembered an item which had pleased him. Keith slid off the window-sill and looked closer.

It was a photograph of Park Lane United, last season's league champions. The whole first team squad of twenty were posed in three lines against an empty grandstand. In the middle, clutching a ball with the date painted on it, sat Jimmy Taylor the captain, flanked by eight other pairs of brown knee-caps and stiffly smiling faces. Six players stood behind him—including two goalkeepers—and behind them, balanced on a bench, were the other five. In their uniform red-and-white strip and with their arms folded at exactly the same angles, the First Division footballers looked remarkably similar, belying the various skills and temperaments which they showed every time they took to the pitch in earnest. Keith, of course, knew many of them, and so did most other boys in the country, for these were the champions. To Donovan, though, they seemed to mean something special.

'This your team?' asked Keith quietly. 'Park Lane?'

There was no reply, just a hard, silent stare at the large photograph. Donovan's brown eyes ran along the line of players. Here and there they paused, or went back for a longer look at a particular face; then two or three men were linked together in a series of glances from one to the other. The Park Lane team seemed to be reviving their moments of glory in his mind. They could almost have been re-running particular moves and patterns of play. It was as if Donovan could hear the players shouting, the whistle blowing, the crowd roaring.

'Great team!' said Keith. 'Better than our lot. ''City East, they're the least''—that's what we shout when they lose. 'Course I've seen Park Lane on telly, but never real. Do you go and see them play?'

He now linked Donovan's North London address with the Park Lane United ground. It must have been Donovan's local club.

'Wish we could draw them down here in the Cup. It's our only chance of seeing them at our ground.' He looked again at the haughty champions. 'We'll never be in the same league. Not in a million years.'

Handling it as delicately as a sheet of thin glass, Donovan laid the big photograph down on the bed. Then with the first hint of determination he had displayed, he got up and went over to the fireplace. Reaching above it to the lifeboat tea-towel, he twisted out the four drawing-pins which were holding it and took it down; he folded it and put it on the chest of drawers. Then with infinite care, like an art collector hanging a masterpiece, he put Park Lane in its place. Donovan stepped back. The twenty men in the team looked out over the bedroom. Donovan stared up at them, the smiling, confident, athletic figures.

The bond between the boy and the picture was so strong that Keith suddenly felt unwanted: in the way, out of place. He sat there for a few moments as the feeling grew in intensity. Then quietly he crept from the room, shutting the door as he went, and walked back down the landing to his own room. He shut his own door firmly, and heaved a huge unhappy sigh. School tomorrow; old Henry's class; Donovan. Frustrated, he looked at his bed, ready to do an almighty dive on it. But before he gave the springs the supreme test, and before his father shouted at him up the stairs, he let forth a curdling high-pitched yell:

'City!'

Just before nine o'clock that evening Mrs Chapman made her final visit to Donovan's room. Both she and her husband had gone up once or twice to see that everything was all right and to tell him what programmes were on the television. But although Keith went down to watch a couple of his favourite programmes before having his cocoa and biscuits, Donovan obviously preferred to remain lying on his bed, staring at the ceiling.

Mrs Chapman knocked at the door going in, balancing a tray carrying Donovan's supper with the other hand. Donovan had not moved. He lay straight on the bed with his hands by his sides—but by now his eyes were closed. Mrs Chapman put his cocoa and biscuits on the small bedside table and gave his shoulder a shake. His eyes opened so quickly it was obvious he had not been asleep.

'Here's your supper, Donovan. I hope you like cocoa; that's what Keith has. If not, I can get you some Ovaltine tomorrow, or Bournvita. It's no trouble.'

There was no reply, but Donovan looked round at the steaming cup. He made no move towards it.

'I know it's not everyone's choice. Mr Chapman says it's too thick. Calls it "a cup of clog".' She laughed. 'But Keith likes it, and Alan used to drink it.'

She found herself talking to him in a sing-song voice she might have used on a four- or five-year-old, talking nonsense for the sake of some sort of conversation.

'Now you get off your bed and drink it up and I'll turn the covers down.'

Obediently Donovan swung his feet round and stood up off the bed. He drank the hot cocoa down and ate one of the biscuits while standing awkwardly by the door.

Meanwhile, Mrs Chapman took off the rumpled candlewick bedspread and turned down the sheets.

'Now, young man, pyjamas. I don't think your dad has packed any, has he?'

She looked at Donovan concentrating on the cocoa in the bottom of the cup.

'Well, I'll get you a pair of Keith's for now, then we must see about getting you some of your own on Saturday.'

Her tone had changed slightly. There was less 'love' and 'dear' in her conversation than there had been earlier in the evening: but she was tired and she found Donovan's lack of response very trying.

When she went into his room she found Keith already in bed.

'I've come for some pyjamas for Donovan,' she said, expecting and getting no reply, and going out with a pair in light blue nylon.

'Here you are, Donovan. Get yourself undressed and into these.' She held them up in front of him for size. 'Yes, they'll do you a treat. Now, along to the bathroom, wash your face and hands and clean your teeth,' she said. 'And you can have a bath tomorrow night.'

She went downstairs to wash up the cocoa things, listening for the sound of water running from the upstairs waste into the drain outside. When she was satisfied she returned. Donovan was in bed, lying as straight under the bed-clothes as he had on top. His black hair and brown face contrasted strongly with the white pillow-case and the sheets. It took Mrs Chapman back to her childhood and the black china doll she had had one Christmas. Donovan looked a sad and lonely figure lying there—in a strange bed in a strange house. Mrs Chapman bent over the bed and kissed him on the forehead.

'Goodnight, love,' she said.

As she went out of the door she noticed the clothes he had taken off folded neatly on a chair. She picked up the pants, the vest, and the socks.

'I'll give these a rub-through,' she said. 'Goodnight.'

With the clothes over her arm and a growing sense of unease in her mind, she once more descended the stairs.

It was eleven o'clock before she roused Mr Chapman from his sleep in front of the wrestling to give him his bedtime cup of tea.

'All right, Doreen?' he asked, coming round. 'Boys all right?'

'Yes, Ted, I think so. I settled Donovan down in a pair of Keith's pyjamas.'

'What about Keith?' asked Ted, sipping the boiling tea. 'Is he happy about this business? He didn't have much to say when he was down here.'

Mrs Chapman did not reply.

'You did snuggle him down, didn't you?'

'Well, I went in and got the pyjamas.' She paused for a moment, thinking. 'But I don't remember kissing him goodnight.'

Without a word the two of them went upstairs and opened Keith's door. The main light was on, and the open football annual showed that Keith had been reading before finally falling asleep.

He was well away, sleeping deeply and peacefully, as far as they could tell. They both kissed him on the forehead and tiptoed out.

'He's all right,' said Mrs Chapman. 'Our Keith understands.'

'Oh, I'm not worried about that,' whispered Ted as they crept into Donovan's room. 'I know he understands. But what does he think of it all? Is it OK with him? That's the question.'

Donovan was sound asleep as well, and the pair of them went back downstairs.

'You know, if he does object we've really got no right to do this.' He stopped and looked his wife in the eye. 'After all, he is our own.'

4

Small groups of children stood about like strangers in the playground. There was little of the charging about and booting of balls that went on during most playtimes and before school. On the first day of the school year everyone was slightly apprehensive. The new Year Six, now the senior group and cocks of the walk, showed the most activity, greeting one another with loud shouts and over-enthusiastic thumps on the back. The rest were very quiet, adjusting to being back in school at all, and taking care of new trousers and dresses. But the quietest clusters of all, here and there attended by older brothers, sisters, and the occasional mum, were the new Year Threes, last year's top infants who were now very much at the bottom of the pile. They resembled young deer on the edge of the herd, unsure and frightened but with heads held high.

Every so often a teacher walked through the playground to be greeted in varying fashions by the different groups. The new Year Six children rarely deigned to speak to other than Year Six teachers, whom they greeted with loud and polite explosions of welcome and wide smiles. There were two or three new young teachers, ignored by all but the few children who rushed to talk to any adult, and both popular and unpopular teachers who walked through to clamorous attention or to total disregard. Mr Bryan was mobbed from gate to steps by all but Year Six, while Mr Henry might as well have been walking across a beach at midnight. Mr Roper was already in the building, having been welcomed shortly after eight o'clock by a few shivering individuals whose parents had gone to work early and turned them out at the same time.

Class members greeted each other after the six-week break in different ways. Some had seen a lot of their particular friends in the holiday, and there wasn't much new to say. Others, not living so close together, welcomed their classmates with restrained delight, everyone talking and no one listening. Nobody spoke to Shemem Parveen, the brightly-clad Asian girl with spiteful fingers, nobody ever did; while Gurdip Singh, the football captain who held a place in the District Side even in Year Five, was met on all sides by warm disciples. Groups of friends, who played together for different reasons, were reunited. The older 'dinner children' formed a tight band, allowing in a few of the sandwich-bringers as hangers on. Children who went home to dinner made up their own gangs, and those who lived near to one another, or who crossed the road together with the lollipop man, somehow stuck together in the playground. All sorts of reasons brought different children together.

There seemed to be little notice taken of anyone's colour; a good brain, a talented right foot or netball arm were what seemed to matter. The exceptions were the few refugee children who spoke poor English. They talked together in a fast foreign language by the school steps: the middle of the playground was not for them.

Keith led Donovan in through the Transport Avenue gate. This was Keith's usual gate, and if he ever missed Dave and Tony on the way to school they always met up here. Keith's eyes scanned the crowded playground for his two special friends. They had grown up through the school from the Infants together and they usually sought each other's company. It was an easy friendship, punctuated by thumps and scuffles, snorts and giggles. There were no rules, no special demands were made on one another except their company. It just seemed a natural grouping, like a small pack of dogs hunting together for a reason which none of them understood.

Dave and Tony were there, just inside the gate as usual. Keith saw them wave and heard the familiar shouts—'Wotcher, Kee!' from Dave and 'Over here!' from Tony. He grabbed Donovan's arm and tried to steer him over towards them. This was important. He badly wanted them all to get on well together. But as Keith turned round, he became, with Donovan, the focus of considerable attention, and he found his way to Dave and Tony barred by an inquisitive group of children from his year. A new boy was worth a glance or two.

''Ere, Chapman. Who's 'e?'

'Is he new?'

Donovan's reaction now was to stare ahead with unfocused eyes. Keith stopped pushing towards Dave and Tony for a moment. He was going to have to say something before he was allowed to get away.

'His name's Donovan. He's living with us. Any objections?'

Nobody objected. Only the older children dared to challenge the strength of the triangle of friendship. Keith and Donovan were now the centre of a little throng. Any friend of Keith's was a friend of theirs, and there was a certain warmth in the circle.

'Hope he's in our class.'

''Ere, mate, are you any good in goal?'

'Is your mum dead?'

The enquiries were necessary to fit Donovan into the order of things, to help them decide their feelings about him. Everyone has a place, and the sooner it is decided and fixed the happier everyone is. Donovan remained silent, so Keith tried to explain.

'His mum's gone back to look after his grandad.'

'Where? Africa?'

'No, Jamaica. But Donovan's living at our house till she gets back. He's, like, my foster-brother.'

The words 'foster-brother' carried sufficiently over the gathered heads to reach the ears of Dave and Tony, alert as ears always are to news which might affect the hearers. Neither of the boys spoke, but the beginning of a sneer wrinkled Dave's nose and a meaningful glance passed between the two boys, now left standing on their own.

The group round Keith and Donovan fell silent as they took in the full meaning of the boy being foster-brother to Chapman.

'Foster-brother?' queried Len Andrews.

'Yes, foster-brother,' replied Keith shortly, trying to bring the questioning to an end. He'd had enough now and he wanted to meet up with Dave and Tony. He spelt it out slowly. 'He's my foster-brother.'

'Is he?' said a voice from the throng. 'Is that why you don't want to know us any more? You got a new black brother.'

Keith swung round at the sound of the familiar voice. He knew before he looked that it was Dave.

Suddenly Keith found it hard to breathe. His heart thumped and his chest went tight.

'Shut up, Dave,' said Tony, who was standing with an arm round Dave's shoulder. 'Don't be rotten.'

Dave coloured a little before Keith's white, angry, and betrayed stare.

'Watch it, Smith,' Keith managed to hiss out, 'or I'll put one on you!'

Dave broke away from the crowd.

'Oh, come on, Tone,' he shouted. 'Let's go. I'm scared stiff.'

He suddenly swung back on Keith. 'But I'll tell you,

Chapman, when you get fed up with little black brother don't come running back to be friends with us! If you're too busy for us today you can bloody stay like it.'

With a backward glance Tony followed Dave away, and some of the others went with them. A few minds were suddenly being changed as it became obvious that Keith could no longer draw strength from Tony and Dave.

'See you later,' said one, not sure yet, as he drifted away. Keith and Donovan might make a formidable partnership on their own.

'Just don't forget your old mates, Chapman,' said another, an emboldened boy who had never claimed Keith's friendship. Then someone at the back of the circle shoved everyone forward, but a heavy plastic ball kicked by one of Year Six landed in their midst and scattered the group, some to chase it and others to avoid the footballers, and the tension went out of the situation.

'Let them get on with it,' said Winnie Marshall, one of the few girls in the group. 'What's it all about anyway, Keith?'

Keith pulled a face. 'I dunno,' he answered.

And truly, he didn't.

Mr Henry was on the whistle.

'Just my fortune on the first day of term,' he had complained in the staffroom. 'It needs one of the women to sort these blessed infants out.'

Nevertheless, at five minutes to nine he stood on the stone steps which led from the playground into the lower hall and gave a long, shrill blow on his plastic whistle. The response was typical of the first day of term; it was immediate. Everyone stopped running, most stopped talking, and the assembled playground turned to face the school. Later on in the term it would be different: a series of whistlings and a variety of coaxes and threats would be necessary, especially by the younger teachers, before order was achieved. But now there was silence, and no movement. Wisely, Mr Henry decided to get rid of the likely source of trouble first. He pulled himself up to his full five feet seven, straightened his tweed jacket like an officer on parade, and bellowed his first order.

'I want all you new ones, you infants, to walk quietly into school and wait for Mrs Pressnose in the lower hall.'

This lady's unfortunate name brought a relieved smile and a small titter to the new children as they walked forward to the steps. One of the first to reach them, a white-faced little girl with blonde pigtails, suddenly presented Mr Henry with some flowers she had been carrying for her new teacher. He accepted them with a smile, then changed his stance to the 'at ease' position, holding them out of sight behind his back.

One by one he called the classes into school by age until he reached his own class. 'My new class stand firm,' he shouted, and then went on through the others to the end until thirty-odd individuals were left, scattered over the otherwise empty playground. A small bunch of mothers retreated to the gate, and the first fluttering sweet-papers of the term chased about the tarmac. Mr Henry began to relax.

'Now, my class,' he yelled, 'advance to the steps and be recognized.'

Slowly the children shuffled into a group beneath their new teacher. They stood looking up at him, apprehension on some of the faces; for the past week or so, as the new term drew nearer, they had wondered and worried about the notorious Mr Henry.

He was a scrupulously neat and tidy man. His thinning hair was brushed down flat, his neatly clipped military moustache treated like a pet. Above a pair of well-pressed cavalry twill trousers was a smart bright yellow squared waistcoat, and across it, marking the outer boundary of his ample stomach like a parade-ground chain, ran a long droopy silver Albert for his watch.

'Right, let's see what sort of squad we've got this year. Girls, advance to the bottom of the steps.'

Silently the seventeen girls stepped forward. One or two, faces up and smiling, would soon be chattering themselves into the jobs of bringing his tea, changing his calendar, running his errands. But now they stood quietly like the rest, to be looked over. Mr Henry's trained military eye scanned from left to right.

'Yes, you look reasonably like human beings,' he pronounced at last. There was a big, slightly forced, laugh from the whole class. 'Now the boys; let's have a look at you. Up straight!'

The boys threw out their chests and stood to attention like a squad of raw recruits. Their faces were eager and shining. Old Henry didn't seem so bad after all, now that you got to know him.

'Good, good.'

As yet he didn't know one from another, they were just his new class. Their paths might have crossed before, but he was ignorant of any names. Keith looked at Donovan out of the corner of his eye. Donovan's stance and expression had hardly changed since they first came into the playground. He stood with his feet together, his hands hanging down by his sides and his head slightly bowed, facing the steps. His eyes were open, but they were unfocused. Keith looked the other way, to where he knew Dave and Tony were standing. They were very close together, ready like the rest for a favour to fall from Mr Henry. Normally Keith would have been close too, part of the inseparable unit, but now he felt separated by more than the few metres between them. This wasn't at all how he had imagined the beginning of term.

'Well, I'll soon get to know your names, and your characters no doubt,' Mr Henry went on. 'All your strengths . . . ' He paused, and then with greater emphasis, ' . . . and all your little weaknesses.' He looked around him and expanded his theme. 'I'll get to know those who can't add, or can't read, or can't sit still, or can't get up in the morning, or can't do as they're told . . . '

His shafts found homes in various beating hearts as their 'little weaknesses' were catalogued, but being old hands at the business of going to school, they gave nothing away by their faces.

'And now,' concluded Mr Henry to everyone's relief, 'we shall walk into the classroom in a quiet and orderly fashion, beginning the term as we mean to go on.'

He turned abruptly and shouted at the door in front of him, bouncing his voice back to his troops behind:

'Follow me. Girls first, then the boys.' And he marched into the darkened doorway, his posy clutched at forty-five degrees behind his back. Keith's sigh of relief as he went into school was especially heavy: perhaps because it was for two.

Mr Roper invited Keith's mother into his room with a wide welcoming gesture. She had timed her arrival well—five minutes before the time of the interview—and she had sat on one of his waiting chairs at the top of the stairs on the small platform overlooking the hall. The hall hadn't changed a lot since her own schooldays at Transport Avenue. It looked smaller, of course, and the floor was shinier; but it looked less elegant with gymnastic ropes looped from the high ceiling to the walls, and with pull-out wall-bars standing flat across the space where the big picture of King George and Queen Elizabeth had hung. The hall was now painted in pastel blue instead of the regulation brown and cream of her youth, but structurally it was unaltered. At least this school, she thought thankfully, hasn't gone in for pulling down all the internal walls and turning the children loose inside.

Mr Roper's room was a model of neatness and compact efficiency. Along the bedroom-style mantelpiece behind his desk stood a small elegant clock, a flip-over calendar on a stand and a plastic framed mirror from Woolworth's. The calendar was correct, and the clock accurate to the second, while the mirror kept Mr Roper as precisely right as time permitted. His main problem was his hair. He had grown it extra long on the left side of his head so that it could be combed over the high bald dome, but any little flurry of activity, even bending to look at a child's work, could send the whole careful arrangement sliding from its peak like an avalanche. He was always very annoyed when this happened and hurried back to his room at the first opportunity to put things right.

The desk between Mrs Chapman and the headmaster was bare except for a small black telephone, a thick diary, and a notepad. As she spoke he took from his pocket an expensive looking four-colour ballpoint pen. He put it in gear for writing in blue and laid it on the pad in front of him.

'I think my letter explained what it's all about, Mr Roper,' Keith's mother began. 'We're fostering Donovan until his mother returns from the West Indies. It could be one month, it could be six. It just depends how long the grandfather in Jamaica is ill. Donovan's father works long hours and they thought there was a danger that the boy would be left to fend for himself for too long.'

'Yes, I understand,' said Mr Roper, nodding and touching his fingertips together. 'Now what can you tell me about his previous education?'

'Oh, the welfare people said they would be sending you the details of his schooling so far. Apparently he's done quite well at school.' Mrs Chapman paused before continuing. 'But there is one problem which seems to have cropped up.'

'Yes?'

'I'm afraid he won't talk.'

'Ah,' Mr Roper responded. 'Well, that'll make a change in this school.' He chuckled like a vicar at a wedding reception. 'How do you mean?'

'Well, they say he can talk. He usually does talk. Quite normally. But since he arrived at our house yesterday afternoon he hasn't said a word to anyone. He just looks down, or straight ahead, but he doesn't seem to be looking at anything. He does as he's told, he eats his food and he dresses himself. But he doesn't say a word.'

'Hmmm,' said Mr Roper, thinking. 'Well, I expect the psychologists have a name for it. But I wouldn't mind betting it's just good old-fashioned shyness. He'll come round. Give him a day or so and we won't be able to stop him gabbling on.'

He stood up to let Mrs Chapman know that the interview was over.

'Don't worry about it, and don't let him feel that you're anxious.'

Mrs Chapman stood up too.

'Yes, of course,' she said. 'I didn't send a note to his teacher about it. I thought I'd tell you. But I do think Mr Henry ought to know.'

'Quite right, Mrs Chapman, quite right,' said Mr Roper as he steered her to the door a little impatiently. There was much to do this morning and there was a staff-meeting at dinner-time. 'I'll pop in and tell him myself. Rest assured, everything will be all right.'

Mrs Chapman thanked the headmaster and left the building. He seemed confident enough about it, she thought. And as long as the boy's teacher knew about the problem there was no reason why she should worry unduly for a couple of days. She put the problem out of her mind for an hour or so and went off to do the shopping.

5

Mr Henry had a pet routine with the register which he liked to follow. Instead of calling each child's name in turn and waiting for the answering voice, or silence, he gave each child a number which corresponded with his or her place on the roll. Then, at registration times, the children simply called out their numbers in turn, with Mr Henry stroking in the squares in red ink, and glancing up briefly before calling out the missing number himself in the case of an absence. With a well-drilled class it became a swift and efficient method of marking the register.

On the first day of term, of course, some little time had to be spent in allocating numbers and explaining the system to the class. Mr Henry was quite prepared for that. He could be very patient over the matter providing it enabled him to mark the register swiftly without any unsightly mistakes. He took a pride in keeping a perfect register.

This morning the open register lay on the desk in front of Mr Henry together with his matching red and black fountain pens. After seating everyone at a separate desk in rows and by sex, each child a little island, Mr Henry began to teach the register technique. Keith had managed to get in behind Donovan, but Tony and Dave were split, and way over on the other side of the room the girls were missing their particular friends too. It was very different from the grouped work-tables of Miss Davis's class.

'It's a simple system,' Mr Henry explained, 'and an

efficient one. You merely remember your own number and call it out in order. But I only allow three seconds for waking up. If you waste my time I waste yours, and you remain behind at the end of the day for extra work. All clear? Right, now the numbers.'

The class sat up, eyes unblinking, ears cocked like hunting dogs' in case they should miss the vital number.

'Andrews, Leonard, number one.'

Andrews, Leonard, smirked. He was used to being Len. Leonard, Andrews or Leonard Andrews. But he had never been back to front before.

'Arthurs, Mark, number two.' Another smirk. 'Bamrah, Anjit, number three.'

Mr Henry sounded the name out slowly, like a child with a hard book. Ranjit Singh Bamrah grinned. 'Bamrah' was the family name normally reserved for marriage purposes—but there were too many Singhs and he had to be fitted to the English pattern somehow.

'Bell, Dennis, number four.' Mr Henry looked up with a heavy twinkle and added, 'Or should that be "Bell, Ding-Dong, number four"?'

The class, including Dennis, laughed. It wouldn't be the last time Dennis had to laugh at one variation or another of that same joke. He had great sympathy for Mrs Pressnose.

'Chapman, Keith, number five. Croft, Donovan, number six. Delmonte, Gino, number seven . . . '

The names and the numbers were read through to the end. So far, so good. But with Donovan's name coming so close to the head of the list Keith knew that trouble could not be far away.

Donovan was sitting in his desk like a prisoner in court, head slightly bowed and hands held neatly in his lap. From behind, Keith could imagine how blank the expression was on his face. It was all he had seen since the boy arrived. He showed not the slightest interest in anyone or anything. His eyes were glazed as if he were hypnotized and his mouth remained firmly closed. All Keith's attempts to get some answer from him, all Keith's parents' attempts, all the children's attempts, had met with the same stone wall of silence. But Keith reckoned it couldn't last for much longer. Sooner or later Donovan would have to answer old Henry, and talk to him in class, or there would be an almighty row. This register business would be the first trial. Donovan might just as well be sensible and start now by calling out his number. It wasn't much to ask.

While Mr Henry was sorting out the pronunciation of a girl's name at the end of the list, Keith slid forward on his chair so that his feet were within kicking range of Donovan's ankles. He lunged forward. After two misses Keith made contact. Donovan must have felt the sharp rap on his heel but he did not move. Keith tried again, harder, and nearly fell off his chair in the attempt. But still Donovan would not respond. He didn't move a muscle. Keith muttered something dark, sinister, and nasty to himself and decided to try another approach. He shifted his weight and leaned his body as far forward over his desk as he could until he was a few centimetres from the back of Donovan's head.

'Say your number!' he hissed economically. 'Say your . . .'

'Is that lad talking over there?' boomed Mr Henry, swivelling in his chair to face Keith. Cut short and caught squarely, Keith's face filled with a deep red as rapidly as a character in a cartoon film.

Mr Henry fixed Keith with a beady eye. He spoke almost without moving his lips.

'One lesson to learn in my class, laddie, is that when I

am speaking you are silent, and when I am silent you are still silent,' he cautioned. 'That is, unless specific permission is given to the contrary. Is that clear?'

'Yes, sir,' answered Keith.

'Right, then, you lad will remember what I have told you and we shall continue by having a first run-through of the register. You all know your numbers. You all know where your numbers come.' A pause. 'Or perhaps if you don't you'd better revisit the infant school for a few days. Now, all sit up straight and be ready to begin on the word of command.'

He looked round to check that the troops were ready. They were.

'Right. Andrews, off you go, lad. Number . . . ?'

'One,' called Len Andrews.

'Two,' followed Mark Arthurs.

The roll began at a cracking pace. Keith watched Mr Henry closely. He was bent low over his register marking in the squares with a new wooden pencil, in case of mistakes. He was not looking up as the numbers were called. Keith knew he shouldn't have to because there were no absentees.

'Three,' called Ranjit Bamrah.

'Four,' Dennis Bell followed.

Now it was Keith's turn.

'Five,' he called, his heart thumping and a choking feeling rising in his throat. There was a second's pause. Would Donovan be sensible and call out his number? It would be better for him if he did. There was an awful silence, perhaps more apparent to Keith than to anyone else. It went on. Obviously, Donovan was not going to speak.

Keith took a deep breath.

'Six,' he called, deepening his voice and clipping the word short.

'Seven,' sang out Gino Delmonte.

Keith looked up. Mr Henry was still concentrating on the register in front of him as the boys continued to go through the list. Keith breathed a temporary sigh of relief. Trouble had been averted, and he was pleased about that, but he knew very well this couldn't go on for ever. He looked again at Donovan, who hadn't moved an inch in the last ten minutes. He wouldn't be left so unaffected for long.

The roll-call was eventually completed. Mr Henry looked up, beaming.

'Well, that wasn't too bad for the dry run,' he said. 'But I shall be using my pen this afternoon, so on your toes, on your toes.'

His eyes shot over to the back left corner of the room as Dave Smith slowly levered his arm into the air.

'Yes, laddie, what is it?'

'Please, sir . . . '

'Stand up, boy, stand up when you're speaking to me or to the class. It's common courtesy.'

Dave got slowly to his feet, his eyes avoiding Keith's hot stare.

'Yes?'

'Please, sir, Chapman called out Croft's number.'

Nearly everyone else had noticed Keith's impersonation as well, and there was a nasty silence as everyone waited to see what Mr Henry would do.

The teacher looked down at his register, then across at the row of desks containing Keith and Donovan. It seemed a year before he answered. His face gave nothing away, impending anger or likely leniency.

'Ah, some confusion. Well, it seems to have sorted itself out. They're both here and they both have a mark.'

He got up and walked round to the front of his desk,

picking up a blackboard pointer as he went. Then he leaned back against his desk, the pointer horizontal between both hands, and cautioned his squad.

'But I want a good run this afternoon,' he said. 'I'll be watching very carefully for mistakes. Watching very carefully.'

Keith's heart continued to beat in a fast rhythm as the scare worked itself out, before a feeling of relief slowed his pulse. Then fear and relief both gave way to a great aggressive loathing for that swine Smith for telling on him. And another, not much less intense, for that idiot Donovan, who still sat there as if he was in Madame Tussaud's. What a stinking rotten business.

'And now, to gladden your hearts,' Mr Henry announced, 'I have one or two tests to be completed to give me some idea of what you can do. Something that will tell me all about those little weaknesses we were discussing in the playground this morning.'

The groan did not need to be audible to be heard throughout the room.

'Steel, give out the paper.'

He tossed a new packet of paper across to a boy at the front.

'Wide space at the top, narrow space at the bottom. Names on the top line and fold the paper in half.'

John Steel scurried up and down the rows as Mr Henry rattled off the instructions like one who could do it in his sleep (as indeed he did). Then the teacher suddenly lunged at the blackboard and turned it round. Twenty sums faced the class, written in thick white chalk on the freshly blacked board, graded from the addition of tens and units to the subtraction of the area of a roll of lino from the area of a kitchen floor.

'Do as many as you can. No talking, no looking at tables, no questions.'

Mr Henry made sure his message went home with a panoramic look of menace.

'Begin.'

So began the test of mathematical ability, while Mr Henry sat down at his desk and neatly inked over the pencil strokes in the register with bright red ink. The room was quiet, and as the class began work, the pleasant sound of laughter drifted across the hall from one of the other classes.

Keith concentrated on the first question on the blackboard. But not before he had seen with interest that Donovan appeared to be working at the sums already. Well, that was something. It gave Keith sufficient respite to do as well for himself in the test as he could manage. For half an hour or so, he even forgot the explosion that was bound to occur after dinner when the register was called again.

After school dinner Keith told Donovan about Mr Henry. He dragged him away from the mickey-takers and the hangers-on to a fairly private place, the boys' toilet. The surroundings were not ideal, but diplomacy isn't always practised in embassy state-rooms.

'You stupid twerp!' Keith began. 'Do you want bother? If you don't speak to old Henry he'll do his nut. He'll think you're being specially awkward for him. And he can be pretty stroppy himself. So use your loaf. Just talk to him, that's all.'

Donovan stood facing the glazed porcelain, his mouth set in a line as he breathed slowly and heavily through his nostrils.

'You're not deaf, are you?' Keith shouted at him, mad with the silent, unresponsive 'brother' he'd been lumbered with. 'Do you hear me?'

Donovan's only reply was a slow, a very slow, shutting and opening of his eyes.

'Well, you'd better take notice. Or you won't half be in for it this afternoon. And don't think I'm going to help you because I'm not.' He turned away. 'And anyway, I can't,' he added, over his shoulder. 'Old Henry will be watching.'

He walked out of the toilets and leaned against the wall. He was fed up. What a mess. Already he felt ten years older than he had in Miss Davis's class last term. He watched a spirited game of football being played around and through all the other children in the playground. He wanted to join in, but it was pretty hard to get into a game once the sides had been picked up. You needed to bring someone else about as good as you for the other side, or they wouldn't let you in. He thought of getting Donovan, but he knew that would be useless. So he stood and watched the match like a player under suspension, his eyes on the game but his thoughts somewhere else.

If he had gone back into the toilet he might have been surprised to find that Donovan was at last reacting to something. As he stood and used the urinal, two huge tears rolled down his face, and a sob jerked his shoulders.

The tears left pale salty marks down his cheeks, pioneering a trail which many others were to follow.

6

Mr Henry charged into the classroom like a bull into the ring, scattering children who had loitered in the front to the safety of their seats. He threw open the register and whipped his pens from his pocket in two swift movements as he sat down. Sensitive to the danger in the air the class settled quickly into a motionless silence.

'Register!' barked Mr Henry. 'No mistakes.'

Staff-meetings always affected him this way, especially in the lunch-hour on the first day back. The children understood his shorthand speech and sat up ready to call out their numbers when the time came.

Keith's nervousness rolled in his stomach. His heart thumped harder and his lungs ran short of oxygen. He took a deep breath, but it didn't seem to help.

Donovan, in front, was sitting up straight with his hands before him on the desk. There was no way by which Keith and the others might tell whether or not he would play Mr Henry's game. But judging by their sideways glances the whole class was curious to find out.

'All right,' said Mr Henry. 'Up straight and concentrate.'

He held his red pen poised above the long column in the register.

'Andrews?'

Len Andrews began the ritual. 'One.'

'Two.'

'Three.'

The first three boys called their numbers then they

turned in their seats to get a good view of Donovan and Keith. Quick glances at Mr Henry told them that he had not looked up yet, but Keith guessed he was not as engrossed in the register as he pretended.

'Four,' called Dennis Bell, and another thick red line was stroked across a printed square in the book.

Now it was Keith's turn. Mr Henry glanced up from beneath his full grey eyebrows and stared intently at him.

'Five, sir,' called Keith.

His words hung in the silence which followed and they echoed in the bare room. Now everyone was waiting for Donovan. He neither moved nor spoke. It was as if his body was present but his mind was elsewhere. In the silence Mr Henry glanced back to his register and inked in Keith's mark. Keith's heart pounded faster. This was it. He hadn't meant to try again, but without thinking of the consequences he took a wild half chance. Swiftly raising his hand to cover his mouth, he called Donovan's number.

'Six.'

It was a daft thing to do. He could never get away with it. There was an immediate stir in the room, but Dave Smith was the first to give the disturbance a clear voice.

'Please, sir, that was Chapman!' he shouted in triumph from his seat in the corner.

'It wasn't, sir,' Keith began denying hotly, but Mr Henry was already on his feet. In four angry strides he marched down the aisle and stood over Keith.

'I don't know what stupid and insolent game you two are playing,' he shouted at Keith and Donovan, 'but I am not having this sort of behaviour in my class.'

His voice was fast and thin with real anger, as distinct from the slow thunder of his usual acted outrage.

'Stand up!' he commanded Keith.

Keith did so. Mr Henry backed a pace to stand towering over Donovan.

'Stand up, boy!' he repeated.

Donovan slowly got up and stood looking forward through half-closed lids, the picture of what Mr Henry called dumb insolence, his old army term for a man who made clear what he was thinking without saying a word.

'If you idiots think you can get away with this sort of outrageous behaviour in my class you are very much mistaken,' shouted Mr Henry. 'How dare you! How dare you!' he demanded, his hands on his hips, bending forward at the waist. 'What's your name?' he shouted at Keith.

'Chapman, sir.'

'Chapman,' Mr Henry repeated, as if the name was something he had found stinking under his shoe.

He twisted back to Donovan. 'And what's your name?' he shouted.

For a second or so the only sound to be heard was that of Mr Henry noisily replacing his spent breath. Donovan said nothing but remained looking sullenly forward.

'I said, ''What's your name?'' ' shouted Mr Henry, his voice rising a tone higher.

There was still no reply.

'You!' screamed Mr Henry, pushing Donovan's shoulder and almost rocking him off balance. 'What is your name?'

'Please, sir, it's Croft, sir,' said Keith from behind the silent Donovan. 'Please, sir, he can't—'

'I know it's Croft,' cut in Mr Henry, turning and spitting words over Keith. 'You mind your own business!' He swung back at Donovan. 'You, Croft,' his voice screamed even higher, 'what is your name?'

As he spoke he punctuated each of the last four words

with sharp blows to Donovan's shoulder, rocking him harder each time until with the final shout Donovan stumbled back across his chair.

As he regained his balance, his face still closed and secret and his eyes staring ahead, Mr Henry pushed himself round in front of the desk and stared with bulging eyes into Donovan's face. His chest heaved as he gulped oxygen into his system.

'Tell me!' he shrieked, any grip he had had on his temper now slipping completely from him, totally out of control. 'Tell me your name!'

As he raged, he slapped Donovan hard across the face with the palm of his hand.

'Tell me, you stupid black idiot!'

The words stamped themselves indelibly in thirty-six minds as Donovan stood there saying nothing. But the hot tears which rolled down his cheeks told their own story of pain and misery.

'Get out! Get outside the door!' screeched Mr Henry in a last high-pitched attack. 'I'm not having it. I am not having it.'

His voice dropped an octave. He suddenly seemed to regain control of himself as Donovan walked slowly out of his place, down the aisle and out of the classroom door.

'Sit down, Chapman,' he said, his face scarlet. 'You've not heard the last of this. You've not heard anything like the last of this.'

Keith sat down, shaking with mixed feelings of fear and guilt and anger. He was frightened physically of the large man and what he might do with his hands or a cane. His guilt sprang from his attempt to fool the teacher by calling Donovan's number. But these emotions occupied a small part of his feelings compared to the immense anger he felt at Mr Henry's spiteful treatment of the boy.

Back at his own desk, Mr Henry repeated his warning.

'I'm not having it. I am not having it.'

He slammed the register shut and put his pens back in his pocket. His own heart was racing and he felt unwell. He had never, in all his life, been so defied—in front of a squad of men or a class of children. It would take some getting over.

'Get out your reading-books and be quiet,' he ordered the class, 'while I sort this matter out.'

The children opened their desks silently and took out their new reading-books—some to read for short spells and others to turn slowly from picture to picture. As the children began flicking over the pages, Mr Henry thought longingly of the brandy in his silver hip-flask. Of course he dared not get it out of his jacket pocket here in front of the class. It was so near and yet so far. He consoled himself with the thought that he would pour a good measure into his playtime cup of tea.

For a while the classroom was still and quiet. But it was a surface stillness, for as the hands turned the pages the eyes flashed round the room with telegraphed messages. Chapman was for it. So was Croft. Everyone was simply waiting for the next move.

Suddenly there was a knock at the classroom door. The whole class turned to face it in one movement. Mr Henry turned more slowly, more deliberately. The thought running through every head was the same. Was Donovan coming in to apologize?

'Come in!' commanded Mr Henry.

The door opened and a tall girl walked demurely in.

'Please, sir, Mrs Cheff said please could she have your register?'

The room was by now used to heavy silences. But there was none so laden with atmosphere as this long pause.

Finally, 'No!' said Mr Henry brusquely. 'No, she can't.'

Mystified, and not a little shocked, the girl withdrew, leaving the class to their boring books and the most uncomfortable three-quarters of an hour any of them had ever known. Nobody dared move, not even to go to the toilet. It was a close thing for some of them. When the playtime bell eventually went it was to as great a feeling of relief as any of them had ever felt in school before. It had been the sort of afternoon nobody ever forgets.

When the class was dismissed, Mr Henry led the way out of the door and hurriedly made for the staffroom stairs. Not at all himself, he ignored a group of children who were romping with a climbing rope in the middle of the hall, and he even apologized to a small boy who bumped into him. Visibly shaken by his brush with Donovan, he raced to the sanctuary of the staffroom.

Donovan himself was nowhere to be seen. Keith shrugged off both sympathy and sneers and hurried after Mr Henry into the hall. When he saw that Donovan was not just outside the door, he looked behind all the projecting buttresses, behind the PE apparatus and at the waiting area outside Mr Roper's room, but Donovan was not to be seen. Keith badly wanted to see him. Where was he? Several possibilities occurred to him. He could have been spotted standing outside the classroom door by Mr Roper and might now be inside his room. He could have gone outside to the toilet, or perhaps to the playground. Or he could have run off. Keith decided that being in with Mr Roper or running off were the two most likely possibilities. Either way, he would have to wait until after play to do anything about it. Meanwhile, he decided to look in the playground in the forlorn hope that Donovan was out there. And if he couldn't see Donovan he had a growing score to settle with Dave Smith.

There was no gradual build-up to Keith's fight with

Dave. Keith went into it suddenly and angrily with no thought for what would happen. He saw Dave standing with Tony in a short queue for water at the fountain by the cellar steps. Their backs were to Keith as they fidgeted in the line and kept bumping the big girl in front. Dave did not see Keith walking fast towards him, nor did he have much warning of what happened. He just heard 'You rotten creep, Smith!' and felt a cold, hard blow on his left ear. The force cracked his head against the school wall and for one or two painful seconds Dave was unable to react to what was going on. In that time Keith had swung at his head again. The second blow caught Dave hard on his left cheek-bone as he turned to face the onslaught, and the hurt spread like spilt acid across the left side of his head.

A sudden spraining pain shot down the back of Keith's hand, swiftly followed by the sting of a blow to his own ear as Dave began punching back. The two boys shouted angrily at each other. Neither of them attempted to defend himself: they were both too angry for that. Wide-armed, wild, with hard-clenched fists they slammed at one another's heads, the blows they received ignored in the scrap to land more on the other. It was hard and bitter, this fight between old friends.

A crowd quickly gathered. First there, and quick to take a patronizing interest, were the Year Six boys. They yelled advice and took their amusement at the same time.

' 'Av 'im, Smith!'

'Kick his crutch!'

'Give him a kiss!'

But when they saw the intensity of feeling in the fight they stopped their scoffing and stood just watching instead. It was the younger ones coming up after who started the next wave of shouting, the traditional chant which brought everyone running.

'Fight! Fight! Fight! Fight! Fight!'

A misplaced blow at Keith's mouth signalled the beginning of the end of it. One of Dave's punches was parried by Keith, not in defence but through a collision of limbs, as Keith aimed a blow at the top of Dave's head. The fist glanced off Keith's forearm and almost the full force of the punch went on to sink into Keith's throat, full on his Adam's apple.

No fighter can go on without wind, and nothing stops breathing quicker than a chop to the throat. Within two seconds Keith was reduced to a choking open target, his arms down, his head swaying to and fro in a frantic struggle for air. Dave took a step back to deliver the final blow. He pulled back his right arm, re-clenched his fist and took aim at Keith's nose. There was a sudden silence from the crowd. This was the climax. Everyone was waiting.

'Stop it!' thundered a voice in Dave's ear, shouted from such close quarters that Dave smelt, although he couldn't name it, the sweet heavy smell of Napoleon brandy on the shout. Mr Henry had hurried late from the staffroom to do his playground duty.

Keith was bent double, coughing and spluttering, supported by the wall, the sound of his suffering drowned by a loud groan from the crowd denied the final blood-letting.

'You again, Chapman?' the teacher shouted, enraged enough to ignore the first need of the boy fighting for breath against the wall. 'I've just about had enough of you today. Get up to Mr Roper. Immediately.'

He turned to Dave, whose name he could not remember. 'And you, lad. Get up there and tell Mr Roper why I sent you. For fighting,' he reminded them unnecessarily. 'Go on!'

Keith, his eyes red and bulging, managed to draw a

couple of shaky, sobbing breaths. Still using the wall as a support he drew himself up—all but his head, which remained drooping forward.

Dave stared at him with angry eyes.

'Please, sir, he started it, sir,' he said, vehemently pointing a long straight arm at Keith. 'He just came up and hit me for nothing.'

Mr Henry turned away. 'I'm not interested,' he replied. 'You can explain yourselves to Mr Roper. Now get off upstairs.'

The whole school had gathered round the fight except for a few girls and a group of younger boys who were enjoying the unaccustomed space for football. But the throng parted like the Red Sea as Keith and Dave walked towards the school steps. Dave walked quickly, indignantly, the innocent party wrongly arrested. Keith followed more slowly, his head still down, his hand to his tender throat as he breathed painfully.

They did not speak to each other, even when they were alone together outside Mr Roper's door. Dave stood and stared at the door, bristling with readiness to explain his innocence. Keith waited further back, breathing more easily now, scarcely believing the truth of this nightmare. He looked down across the hall at Miss Davis's classroom and thought longingly of that last summer: the games of rounders in the hot playground, the outing up the river to Hampton Court, the laughs in class, the friendship with Dave and Tony. This last thought choked him most of all. In the space of two days Donovan had destroyed that, and now school was the sort of unpleasant place it had been for his dad. Perhaps it's like this for everyone as they grow up, he thought.

The door to Mr Roper's room suddenly opened and Keith swung round nervously. But it was the school secretary Mrs Cheff with a pile of registers and tobacco tins of dinner-money. She gave the boys one of those looks which only school secretaries can to pupils in trouble—a mixture of surprise, disappointment, and sympathy.

'Mr Roper won't keep you long,' she said formally. She lived in the same street as Dave and usually smiled at him. Now she disappeared into her little converted cupboard along the landing. Keith sighed and waited.

A sidelong glance at Dave revealed that he, too, was feeling nervous. He had begun biting his thumbnail.

Keith thought about what Mr Roper would do. But it was hard to forecast. Sometimes he would spend a long time just talking to you—like when Johnny Raven was caught smoking in the toilets. At other times he would rant and rave and keep you in for a couple of playtimes. Occasionally, if he was very angry, or if a teacher was really upset about what had happened, he would give you the stick—one on each hand. Some said that getting the stick also depended on whether or not he was pushed for time. Caning was quick, and he didn't have to say much. Keith sighed again. He reckoned he'd be lucky to get away without the stick, with old Henry worked up the way he was.

By now the children were coming into school from the playground and both boys moved further out of sight away from the edge of the landing, nearer to the door. It surprised them both when it was suddenly opened. Mr Roper must have been 'buzzed' by Mrs Cheff on the telephone.

'Come in,' he said sternly. He looked at their puffy red faces, their damp hair, their shirts pulled out. 'You know my feelings about fighting in the playground.'

The two boys went in and stood, literally, on the mat. It was a maroon island, about a metre by a metre-and-a-half, in front of the desk. The obvious and natural thing was to go and stand on it, although it wasn't unknown for

Year Three children, just up from the Infants, to make themselves comfortable in the visitor's chair.

'Well?' asked Mr Roper, shutting the door firmly and returning to his own side of the desk. 'I don't expect to see you two up here. What started all this off?'

'Please, sir, it was Chapman,' said Dave. 'He hit me on the ear for nothing, and Mr Henry sent us up.'

'Is that true, Keith?' asked Mr Roper. 'Did you start it?'

Keith looked down at his scuffed shoes on the maroon carpet.

'Yes, sir,' he replied in a low voice.

Mr Roper was surprised to get an admission of guilt so quickly. He usually had to send down for a witness.

'Oh, well then. You'd better tell me why.'

'Please, sir, he told on me in class, to Mr Henry. Twice,' said Keith, looking up and beginning once more to feel more indignant than frightened.

'I never, sir,' chipped in Dave quickly.

'About what, pray?' asked Mr Roper, slowly.

'About Donovan, sir. Donovan Croft.'

'What about Donovan Croft? What did he do?' questioned Mr Roper, sitting down. This was getting complicated, and very soon he'd have to call a halt, give them a few words on living together in peace and send them packing.

'Donovan Croft can't talk, sir, and I answered his register number for him and Smith told on me to Mr Henry.'

'I didn't, sir.'

'And what did Mr Henry say?' asked Mr Roper, beginning to take a real interest. He began to feel apprehensive as it suddenly dawned on him that Mr Henry never had been given the message about Donovan Croft.

'Please, sir, he . . . '

'Well, go on . . . '

'Please, sir, Mr Henry hit Donovan and stood him outside and he told me off.'

Mr Roper was out of his chair as if a small electric charge had been passed through it.

'Is this true, David?'

'Yes, sir, but I didn't really tell . . . '

Mr Roper rushed round to the door.

'Where's Donovan now? In class?' he demanded.

'No, sir, he's gone. I couldn't find him anywhere,' answered Keith.

'Ye gods,' groaned Mr Roper. 'Stay here, Keith. David, clean yourself up and get back to your class . . . ' and he hurried down his small flight of steps, dodging the swinging bodies of a dance lesson, across the hall to Mr Henry's classroom.

Mr Henry's class was doing an arithmetic test from a tattered set of *New Junior Arithmetics, Book Three, Without Answers*. They thought it most unfair after play in the afternoon. But it had been a peculiar day and nobody quite knew what would happen next.

Mr Henry sat at his desk pretending to sharpen pencils with his silver penknife. They were a new issue and all he did was shower his desk with a lot of black carbon dust. He mostly stared into the middle distance, thinking about what had happened.

He guessed that Croft had been seen by Mr Roper and was in his room getting a ticking-off. Had he not been on playground duty he would have been to see Mr Roper himself—but now he would wait five minutes until the class were well set on their work. He wouldn't mention hitting the boy, except to say (if necessary) that he had tapped him as one would tap a hysterical person, or someone suffering from shock.

He had a shock himself when Mr Roper suddenly walked in.

'Could I have a word with you, please?' asked the headmaster from the door, his signal that he wanted to speak to a teacher out of the eager earshot of the children.

'Yes, certainly, sir,' said Mr Henry with a false confidence. He turned to the class. 'Class, no noise now; I shall only be outside: any sound from you will be a sign of rudeness to Mr Roper and to myself.'

The children looked knowingly at one another, swift to smell misfortune. They knew old Henry should never have hit the new boy, and they knew that Mr Roper had come to sort it out. They'd had mums and dads coming up to the school over things like this before.

In the school hall, Mr Henry drew himself up as tall as he could and looked up at Mr Roper. The two or three inches' extra height which the headmaster possessed counted for something like a foot in this situation. Mr Henry wasn't to know that Mr Roper was himself feeling very guilty for not passing on Mrs Chapman's vital message about Donovan. Agitated at his own negligence, while clearly displeased with Mr Henry, Mr Roper ineffectually pushed a fallen strand of hair back over his bald head and prepared to pitch his voice above the haunting cowboy music of the dance lesson. As he opened his mouth to speak, a girl in a shiny pink slip and black plimsolls gyrated between them, and he changed what he was about to say.

'We'll go to my room. Your class will be all right for five minutes.'

Mr Roper threaded his way back through the children while Mr Henry skirted the floor. Eventually, with Keith and the music shut out of the room, Mr Roper began again.

'Mr Henry, I should have delivered a message to you this morning, about Donovan Croft,' he said, clearing his own conscience first. 'Mrs Chapman, who is fostering him, told me that he has not spoken since he arrived at her house yesterday. We don't know why. I should have warned you that he might be difficult for a few days—and I apologize for not doing so, Mr Henry.'

Mr Henry's eyes widened and he took in a short, sharp breath. A nervous flutter attacked his stomach and he gave a silent, mental groan. Just my luck, he thought, to have to pick a head case. His nervousness began to give way to a feeling of anger. Even forgetting to pass on the message left the headmaster more or less in the clear, but it made a very awkward situation for him. Outwardly, however, he remained unmoved. He waited silently in the visitor's chair. His hands on his knees like an accused officer at a court martial.

Mr Roper continued. 'What I did not realize was that my failure to deliver the message would lead to this.' He cleared his throat. When he began again his voice was deeper and quieter. 'Mr Henry, is it true that you hit the boy for not speaking?'

Mr Henry stared straight ahead.

'I did hit the boy, Mr Roper, but not for not speaking. It was more for insolence—dumb insolence. I'm afraid his sullen and insolent attitude made me lose my temper. I'm very sorry, sir.'

He decided it would be better to be truthful—or almost truthful. There was no need to drag in the business of what he had called the boy.

For the second time that afternoon Mr Roper was grateful that he had no cross-questioning to do, no sorting of the truth from two conflicting stories.

'Thank you for being frank,' he said. 'I can't condone what you've done, and I can't say what the outcome will be. But I think I can understand what made you lose control of yourself. Now I'll be frank. Quite honestly, my action as far as you're concerned will depend on what happens in the next few hours.'

Mr Henry looked surprised. What was Roper driving at?

'You may not have realized it, Mr Henry, but the boy Croft is missing, presumably run home.'

Mr Henry gave another silent inward groan.

'We'll have to make sure of that. But if Mrs Chapman decides to make a fuss I must deal with it. If she wants your blood I shall be very awkwardly placed to defend you—although, of course, I'll do my best to smooth things over. The important thing is to find Croft. I'll send Keith Chapman home to find out if he's there. Meanwhile, you search the school downstairs—toilets, cloakrooms, playground, shelters—and I'll look in all the classrooms up here.'

'Yes, of course,' said Mr Henry, getting up.

Mr Roper made for the door. 'Oh, but wait a minute,' he said, stopping suddenly in the middle of the room, hand to mouth.

'Yes?'

'What does this boy Donovan look like?'

Mr Henry stared into the headmaster's face. He couldn't prevent a faint smile of satisfaction from appearing at the corners of his mouth.

'Don't you know what he looks like? Haven't you seen him?' he asked, as if he'd found a weakness. It was probably unreasonable but it did seem strange to him that after making all this fuss the headmaster hadn't even seen the boy yet.

'No, he came in with Keith Chapman at nine, and Mrs Chapman saw me later,' explained Mr Roper. 'I should have met him when I gave you the message. But, there, we know all about that,' he added awkwardly. 'Anyway, what's he wearing?'

Mr Henry cast his mind back, but it wasn't difficult. The sight of Donovan Croft standing insolently at his desk was etched on his memory.

'White T-shirt, grey trousers, quite tall for my class.'

Mr Roper nodded at each item, signifying that he was taking it all in.

'Is there anything else I ought to know?'

'Oh, yes, there is one thing: he's . . . ' Mr Henry searched for the right word. 'He's black.'

'Yes,' said Mr Roper. 'Thank you. I know.'

7

Mrs Chapman was surprised and very upset
when she saw Keith standing at the door.

'Oh, my God,' she said, 'whatever's
happened to you?'

Keith still looked bad, his face blotchy with punches
and puffy round the eyes. On top of his fight he had run all
the way home at top speed, not even troubling to hold his
breath past the 'dirty house'.

'Are you in trouble, Keith? Have you run home from a
fight?'

Keith pushed past her into the passage. He leaned
against the wall and spoke to his mother between gasps
for breath.

'It's Donovan . . . he got into . . . trouble . . . he's run
off . . . old Henry hit him and called . . . him names . . .
Mr Roper said . . . is he here?'

'Well of all the . . . ' Mrs Chapman began, but she
stopped herself. 'No, he hasn't come home here. At least,
he's not knocked at the door. But the bell doesn't work. He
might've come and I didn't hear him.'

She hurried out into the dining-room and down into
the kitchen. She went out of the back door to see if he had
come along the alley at the back. But Donovan wasn't
anywhere there. Meanwhile, Keith ran up the stairs. He
looked in Donovan's room. It was empty, the Park Lane
footballers on the wall staring down into the quiet room.
Keith met his mother at the bottom of the stairs. She
already had her white raincoat on.

'Come on,' she said. 'I'm coming up to the school to sort this out with Mr Roper.'

On the way Keith, half-walking, half-running beside his hurrying mother, told her what had happened, right from the beginning when Dave had been rotten to him in the playground to Mr Roper's talk with Mr Henry and the search of the school.

Mrs Chapman spoke more to herself than to Keith.

'It's always the way,' she said. 'You do something for the best and it bounces back in your face. If I'd thought it was going to be like this I'd never have taken him on.'

She walked on swiftly, crossing a busy road clutching Keith's hand and skilfully weaving her way between the slow-moving vehicles. Two streets further on she spoke again.

'Still, somebody's got to help him, poor little devil . . . '

At the school Mr Henry had just completed his search. He took the opportunity in reporting the result to voice an opinion of his own.

'I've covered the whole territory, sir, section by section, and the boy is certainly not on the premises downstairs. And if I may say so, he should never have been here in the first place.' He thought he might as well say this now; attack was always the best way of defending a position. 'Surely, special cases such as his require special schooling, special treatment?'

Mr Roper, who had failed to find Donovan also, was in no mood for a debate about special schools, nor for excuses and recriminations.

'Be that as it may, Mr Henry, our first task is to find the boy. What we decide to do with him after that . . . will have to be decided later. Meanwhile, I think you'd better go back to your class for the last half-hour. But please don't leave the school until I've seen you.'

Feeling like the police suspect told not to leave town, Mr Henry made his way morosely back to his classroom. Mr Roper, preoccupied, paced his room, waiting hopefully for Keith's knock on the door with news that Donovan was safe at home with Mrs Chapman.

When the knock came it was much louder than usual and Mr Roper knew it wasn't Keith. He guessed who it was and what news she was bringing. He opened the door himself. Sure enough, Mrs Chapman was standing there with Keith. Mr Roper took two swift looks. The first was an ordinary anxious look to see if Donovan was standing behind them. He wasn't. The second was a professional look he gave to all parent-visitors when he thought they might have come to complain about something. Were they angry or not? He decided Mrs Chapman was 'dignified angry'—the lady wouldn't lose her temper or shout at him, but she would still let him know politely, without saying it in so many words, that the school had much to answer for.

'Good afternoon, Mrs Chapman, come in, won't you? Keith, just wait a minute.' He ushered the erect woman into the room and closed the door. 'Please sit down, so good of you to come,' he began, making his way to the security of his side of the desk. Mrs Chapman sat down. For a moment there was a silence, then they both spoke at once.

'Mrs Chapman, what can I say?'

'He isn't at home, Mr Roper, and he doesn't know the district.'

Mrs Chapman carried on. Her face was very straight, her voice cold.

'Keith's told me about what happened. I'm very upset about it. I definitely didn't expect anything like this to happen, not after what you said, Mr Roper. I don't know what my husband's going to say . . . '

Mr Roper shook his head. This was the nearest most mothers got to a threat of further action. They always hinted that their husbands were going to go berserk at the news.

'But before anything else,' Mrs Chapman reminded him, 'Donovan's got to be found.'

Mr Roper jumped in quickly. 'I quite agree, Mrs Chapman,' he said. 'We can hold the inquest afterwards . . .'

'Are you sure he's not in school?' she asked.

'Perfectly sure, we've looked everywhere on the premises.'

'Then we must search round the streets,' Keith's mother said, 'and tell the police. The boy doesn't even know our address.'

Mr Roper was on his feet in a flash. He gave the impression of a man able to think on his feet, capable of taking swift decisive action. 'An excellent idea,' he said. He thought for a few seconds, then he spoke.

'I suggest the following plan of campaign,' he said, talking rapidly. 'We will search the area systematically and thoroughly, street by street, using as many of the lads and the teachers as we can.' Mentally he spread his map and used his pointer. 'Mrs Chapman, you, Keith, and several volunteers can search the area to the east and north of the school—Transport Avenue, Central Road, Mervyn Street, and so on, as far as your house. Mr Henry and I will head a search-party on the south and the west side of the school—between here and the High Street. Now, liaison . . . ' He thought for a few seconds more. 'When we get to the Co-op on the corner of the High Street and Power Road, we will telephone your house from the kiosk outside. Then if neither party has found the boy, I will go into the police-station in the High Street and report the whole matter to the sergeant on duty. Now, how's that?'

He looked smugly at Mrs Chapman. He thought it wasn't at all a bad plan. But if he expected acclaim he was disappointed; Mrs Chapman accepted the plan flatly, with one proviso.

'Whatever happens we must tell the police before five o'clock. If we don't find him we must give them good warning before it gets dark. Remember, this boy doesn't know the area.'

Mr Roper knew only too well how vulnerable a child could be, alone in a strange district. Only that summer they had lost a non-English-speaking refugee boy in Trafalgar Square. When they found him ten minutes later he was crouching down in terror behind one of the lions; and he didn't stop sobbing until the party saw the turrets of Transport Avenue School again.

'Yes, of course. A good idea,' he said.

Within five minutes the boys and girls from the Year Six classes with Mr Henry's class were assembled in lines in the hall. Mr Roper, leaning over his balustrade, spoke to them from above, while Mrs Chapman stood awkwardly behind him, unaccustomed to being up on a platform. Mr Henry walked up the steps to join her, followed by the Year Six teachers, while Mr Roper told the children about Donovan's disappearance and the part they might play in finding him. He reminded them that they might have seen him with Keith that morning—many of them said they had—then he asked Mr Henry to give a description of the boy. The children stood, silent and important, aware of the real-life drama of the situation.

'The boy is of average height for his age—about as tall as most of you—wearing a white T-shirt and grey trousers. And he is from Jamaica.'

'Black,' one boy told his neighbour, catching on to an important feature.

'In a white shirt,' underlined the other.

Mr Roper leaned forward again. 'He is on his own, and he is probably very nervous and frightened,' he added. 'Should you see him please tell one of us.' He waved a hand behind him to indicate the adults on the platform. 'We won't be more than a street away from you. Now then, when you go out into the playground . . . '

Mr Roper was about to go into the details for splitting up when Mrs Chapman came up behind him and whispered in his ear.

'I think you ought to warn them about his not speaking,' she said. 'In case they don't know.'

Mr Roper nodded. 'Yes, thank you. I think most of them know, but I'll remind them anyway.' He turned back to the children. 'There is one important thing, everyone,' he told the fidgeting hall. 'Donovan is not very well at present. He will probably ignore you when you speak to him. He won't answer you . . . '

' 'e's dumb,' said Dennis Bell.

'Yes, that's right, lad, Donovan is dumb. Or we might say ''mute'',' he corrected, not sure if a difference in meaning existed, but preferring 'mute' because it had a medical ring. 'That means he can hear you and understand you although he may not speak to you. So be very kind and sympathetic to him.'

Mr Henry cleared his throat. He got the message.

Mr Roper continued. 'All right, I'll leave your teachers to give you the details. Then off you go and keep your eyes open. You'll need your wits about you to find him in these busy streets.'

Under the direction of their teachers the excited children filed out of the hall into the playground where they were to be divided up for the search. As they did so, Mr Roper turned to Mr Henry.

'I hope to goodness this works, Mr Henry,' he

muttered. 'If we don't find him I'm afraid we're both going to look very foolish.'

Mr Henry nodded, but he said nothing. He felt something more than foolish already.

Mrs Chapman thought there was a chance that Donovan had headed in the general direction of their house, but that he had missed the turning and was wandering about in a parallel street somewhere nearby. Instead of taking the direct route home, therefore, she went up Central Avenue and then back to the school down the parallel Mervyn Street to satisfy herself that he was not in that area. Partnered by Keith on the opposite pavement she was walking back up Central Avenue for the second time to begin the next part of the search when she realized that this time there would be five possible routes to cover—two off Central Avenue and three off Mervyn Street—and that as she went further from the school the possibilities would multiply upon themselves to such an extent that she would be unable to cover them all before nightfall. She thought for a moment of what her husband had once told Keith about repeatedly folding a piece of paper. If you folded a piece of paper in half and then half again, and could keep on halving and folding what was left, the paper would be doubled and doubled to half a mile thick in no time. As the streets multiplied out in front of her she began to see what he meant. It was an impossible job. She sighed. She would just have to do what she could.

Every so often when the street seemed empty she called Donovan's name, but her cry was hardly loud enough to be heard. She realized that it took more confidence than she possessed to walk down a strange road shouting. But she went down the streets calling softly at intervals and looking into the gardens.

This part of City East had escaped the devastation of

tower-block development. The council preferred to make grants for the existing properties to be improved, a preference applauded by the residents. Each of the houses in the long rows had its own gateway and a small front garden with either a square of cement or a tiny patch of dark and stony grass. Some were shielded by dusty privet hedges, and here Mrs Chapman called, or looked over the gates. Others had basement areas to be peered down into. It struck her that although Mr Roper would have more pedestrians about on the other side of the school, and more shops to deal with, most of the houses there opened out on to the pavement and there weren't so many shaded nooks and crannies to investigate.

There were shops here, of course, but mostly on street corners, and Mrs Chapman couldn't imagine Donovan going into any of them without money, without being able to ask for anything. And the public houses, which shared the corners, were all closed—and barred to Donovan anyway.

Keith tried to keep pace with his mother, but the cars which were parked almost nose-to-tail under the plane trees made it difficult for him to see her most of the time. In any case, he had plenty to keep him occupied. Every so often he would see a small group of people, or someone on their own, who might have been Donovan or a crowd around him. But it always turned out to be a false alarm—perhaps two or three women talking together in the afternoon sunshine, or one of the other children who had run ahead, searching in a disorganized random fashion and giving false hope.

A movement in a doorway suddenly caught Keith's eye. The sun was shining down the street in his face and the porches of the houses were painted black with shadow in the glare. From the depth of the doorway on his left Keith saw what seemed to be the outline of a person of about his own height, with two eyes staring out from a dark face. Could this be Donovan? It was quite possible. But far from being pleased at making a discovery Keith suddenly felt strangely afraid, like he did when he found the person he was looking for in hide-and-seek motionless and staring at him. He didn't want to go any nearer. Instead, he looked the other way, across the road towards his mother; but she had gone on, and through the dusty windows of a parked car Keith could see her talking to a group of women by Fewster's, the corner shop.

Keith jumped when the door on his left slammed. He quickly looked round again at the porch. His eyes squinted against the strong sun into the shadow, but he could see no one there, only a dark brown door with a picture of a ship in it in coloured glass and a bag hanging up in the corner for a tradesman. Keith's first thought was that the boy must have gone in. Then his imagination raced. He could have been pulled in. The local paper was full of unpleasant happenings in the streets of City East. Or perhaps he hadn't been there in the first place. It was hard for Keith to decide what to think, so he resolved to say nothing about it at all.

His mind was taken off the incident by more sudden noise and movement as a group of chanting children came running down the pavement behind him. They were all members of the Transport Avenue search-party from Keith's class, but they weren't searching very thoroughly.

'Seen him, Chapman?' someone asked, trotting past.

'No.'

'Nor us. See you.'

With happy faces and a skip in their step they carried on, chanting rhythmically down the street. When Keith listened he could make out their shout:

'Donovan. Donovan Croft.

Where you bin? Why you lost?'

The words had a different rhythm from any traditional London street cry. This shout had twin roots—in cold football crowds and the hot Caribbean—and round the next corner the children would very likely change it as new words suggested themselves.

Keith looked after them and wished he could go with them. They could run round the streets a couple of times and then run home. He looked both ways behind a parked Rover and ran across to Fewster's corner to find out what street they would be covering next. He sighed. Lucky kids. There'd be no skipping off for him. This had to be done, but his throat still hurt, he had a headache and his legs weren't any too steady. And he couldn't help feeling they wouldn't find Donovan anyway.

On the other side of the school, Mr Roper was meeting with no greater success. He had managed to shake off a group of six big girls who wanted to search with him and tell him about their holidays as they walked—he got rid of them by giving them specific shops to look in along the High Street and down Power Road. But once on his own he began to realize how useless he was. A neighbouring school had come out, probably a bit early, he thought, and there were too many strange children about. Not having met Donovan he couldn't tell one strange boy from another. All the white boys could be ruled out, as well as all the Asians and the boys walking or talking in groups. But that still left a few black boys on their own who could have fitted Donovan's description. As the headmaster of a large school where children joined and left each week, Mr Roper was used to having to look for quick clues as to which children belonged when he met them in the street—a smile or a coy look perhaps—but that was not enough in this situation. Donovan Croft wouldn't know him even if he met him.

It was quite possible that he had walked straight past him already. After a while, frustrated with his own uselessness, Mr Roper stopped looking for the unrecognizable Donovan and kept an eye open instead for one of his own search-party who might know the missing boy; but he was almost at the High Street before he met Ruth Wild and Manjit Kaur, and even they only thought they knew what Donovan looked like. It was doing no good at all for his blood-pressure, nor for the important search in hand. What a day! he thought.

The best attempt to find Donovan was made by Mr Henry. With his military training he brought expertise and experience to the task. First he selected his troops—the boys from his own class the year before—and then he briefed them carefully on the plan of campaign. It took him back to the old days in the Regiment and he did it with mixed feelings of pleasure and nostalgia.

'This is a search and detain operation of the kind familiar to British troops in hostile towns,' he explained. 'The object is to cover the area thoroughly, working to a plan, and to flush out the quarry without giving any warning of approach and without upsetting the general public.' It sounded like a page from a military manual. 'It calls for skill, tact, and discipline. Above all, it requires a clear head and a cool brain.'

The boys stood and drank it in. This was great. If only he had organized a few things like this when they had been in his class.

'There is no room for individual initiative,' he went on. 'We're not seeking medals for ourselves: so don't go chasing off in all directions like flies in a colander.'

George Burch sniggered at Ronnie Hazlehurst. His dad said something different.

'We will proceed street by street in fours, two on each side of the road. Each group of four (which we'll call a "unit") will meet at every crossroads. The first crossroads, Cheshire Avenue, we'll call "Objective One". When a street divides and goes two ways, so does the unit, into pairs: if it sub-divides again so do the pairs. Now listen for your units and your list of objectives . . . '

The boys were divided up and given further instructions on reporting back to mobile platoon headquarters (Mr Henry). Then long after the others had all left, their search began. As a result of their briefing, the boys were well-disciplined and thorough: there were no skipping-chants as they progressed, they were not bewildered by the ever-increasing number of streets to cover, they had no nagging doubts about their usefulness. It was a good search, and it yielded a quick find.

One unit of four had not gone very far down Union Road when a still figure sitting in the back of a parked car, staring ahead with a fixed trance-like expression, attracted the attention of the two boys on the left-hand pavement. Mr Henry's description of the missing boy was matched perfectly: dark skin, short black curly hair and, judging from the shoulders, which was as far down as they could see, with a white T-shirt on. They called the other boys over with whistles and staccato shouts.

''Ere! Over 'ere!'

'What?'

'It's 'im—Donovan—in that car!'

'Is it?'

'Yeah, look, it must be, mustn't it? 'E's black, with a white T-shirt, and look how 'e's sitting, all funny.'

'Yeah.'

'It must be.'

'Yeah.'

The boys walked up to the car, trying to look normal, but the slight forward thrust of their bodies showed how ready they were to pounce. The face in the car remained motionless, mouth slightly open, eyes still staring vacantly ahead. One of the boys remembered Mr Roper's caution.

'Go steady. Don't scare him. He can't talk, remember.'

They crept up to the car and peered in through the windows at their quarry. It was then that the music from the car radio filtered through to them. They were just beginning to wonder what the dickens Donovan was doing sitting in a car listening to the radio when their eyes took in more detail. They immediately saw their mistake. It was a girl. She was probably a few years older than themselves, with a big bust and a long scarlet skirt. Her fingers were flicking to the rhythm of the radio music. As the boys stared in she looked round at them, scared at first, then outraged.

'Push off, you nosy pilks!' she shouted. 'Or I'll get my boyfriend to you!'

With loud shouts of surprise and whoops of derisive laughter, the boys ran off down the road to continue their search. It hadn't been Donovan, but at least it would be something to talk and laugh about afterwards.

They were secretly slightly discouraged, but they were still thorough, and like the rest they looked in and out, high and low: behind walls, into shops, through cars; they stopped and asked; they sent runners to report their progress to headquarters; and when they finally converged on Mr Roper and Mr Henry outside the Co-op, they could say with some certainty that Donovan had not slipped through their net.

Unfortunately, it turned out that he must have slipped through someone's, for no one else had anything to report either. Clearly, he'd got through the mesh—or he was away outside the area of the search before it even began.

As the children finished searching their streets, the clustering throng in the Co-op doorway grew larger. Mr Roper saw the manager looking out through the plate-glass doors with a mixed look of curiosity and complaint. Quickly, the headmaster dismissed the children and consulted with Mr Henry and the other teachers. There was very little for him to say, and only two things left for him to do.

'Well, it only remains for me to telephone Mrs Chapman and find out if the other party have had better luck. If they haven't, then I must inform the police.'

After borrowing a two pence piece from one of the others, Mr Roper went inside the kiosk on the pavement's edge and dialled the number he had previously scribbled in the back of his diary. At the second attempt he got through and pushed the two pence home to stop the annoying pips in his ear.

'Mr Chapman speaking.'

'Oh,' said Mr Roper, obviously surprised. He had expected Mrs Chapman. He didn't feel ready to talk to her husband yet. 'I wonder, is Mrs Chapman home yet? I'm afraid we've had a spot of bother.'

'I think you still have, Mr Roper,' replied Mr Chapman grimly. 'My wife has just called in and told me about what happened. There's no sign of him round here.'

'Oh dear,' said Mr Roper. He sighed deeply. 'Well, I'll have to inform the police, I'm afraid. We had hoped to sort it out ourselves, but we must involve them now— unfortunately.'

'Yes, I think we must, Mr Roper. This is a very bad business all round.'

Mr Chapman stopped there. He would have more to say later, much more.

'But hang on where you are for ten or fifteen minutes,' he suggested. 'I'm going to get my bike out and have a look round the streets on that. Give me your number and I'll ring you back in a quarter of an hour. If I draw a blank you can tell the police.'

'All right,' agreed Mr Roper, the initiative out of his hands now. 'I'll wait here.'

He almost put the phone down.

'Good luck!' he called.

'Yes,' said Mr Chapman. 'Yes. We all need that.'

8

The moist channels of undried tears on Donovan's cheeks were swelled by two large tear-drops. Welling up from the sad depths of his eyes they trickled down to his jaw and wet the front of his T-shirt. He sat on a wooden box in the dusty corner and smelt the sweet aroma of cut cedar.

In his utter misery he thought about home. He had had a home until yesterday. Even though his mother had left them a few weeks ago he had still had a home. It had been a sad home, and lonely when his mother had gone, and life seemed to have come to a stop that day he had woken up to a breakfast prepared by his father; but he had still had a place to come back to, and a father to cry to, and to see crying. Now his father had sent him away, and there was nothing left of the happy days. He was alone and unwanted, and while he cried out for his parents' love again, he felt betrayed by the people he most wanted.

'Where've you gone, Mam? Why've you gone away? I love you and you go away. And I feel bad. I feel real bad.'

Donovan's thoughts were unspoken, but all the same they were meant to be heard, even if the tiny creature he was holding in his cupped hands could not understand them. The little face looked up at him but Donovan did not see it. In the misty, unfocused eye of his mind there was only the picture of his mother, a slim, pretty woman who smiled and loved and drew out from Donovan a love that he could feel. For some white boys, living in a neighbourhood where their parents had grown up, a prominent memory of their mothers might have been of a time when they were comforted over a cut knee or a bruised head. But for Donovan such memories were of times when he had been wounded by words rather than by stones.

'You always loved me. You always kissed me and loved me. When the boys called me names and I cried you said, ''Never mind, boy, we are all the same, and we are all together: your daddy loves you and your mammy loves you: we are all together, and let them call you any old thing.'' Then I didn't cry any more.'

Donovan could think of many times when his mother had comforted him so; when as a little boy he had fallen out with a good friend and been surprised to be called unpleasant names with so much feeling; when, older and more sensitive, other boys who liked him had put an arm round him and affectionately called him racist names instead of Donovan. At these times his mother had kissed him and with sparkling eyes had told him to pay no heed, it was just their way. She had been skilful at making him feel good again, and at showing him that it was his family's own view of themselves that mattered. Much to her annoyance, his father would teach him how to fight the other boys at such times. That, too, helped to turn tears into laughter: for although Donovan was no fighter it was good to be close to his father like that. But deep down he knew it was the arm of his mother that had mattered.

Donovan thought about those times, and about his father. Those fighting romps, and when they went to football together, had been their golden times. Up behind the south goal at Park Lane they talked football and shared sweets and shouted for their favourites. They were keen supporters of the Park Lane team, and knowledgeable about the game. Together they had a Saturday afternoon world of their own. Those had been such good days. But now they were gone, and it was almost impossible for Donovan to bear the sheer physical pain of wanting which was rooted in his stomach.

'Why don't you want me, Dad? Why'd you send me away?'

A low throaty moan, only heard inside his head, accompanied the running of his eyes and the slow unconscious dribbling of his mouth. His shoulders moved in a huge sob, and he almost dropped the small creature which was now curled in his cupped hands. His eyes closed and he gently rocked himself backwards and forwards as if to give himself the comfort he so desperately wanted.

His mind went back to the night of the big row. His parents had been strange with one another for some time. They had begun snapping at one another, they had argued over silly things, they had no longer smiled at one another or touched. It made Donovan feel uncomfortable, but perhaps not so much at the time as looking back afterwards. He couldn't understand why this change should have come over them. All he knew was that his mother had received a letter from Jamaica, and that she had cried a lot when she had read it. They both continued to be very loving to him: his mother gave him more attention than ever, and his father still took him out, even, one unhappy Saturday, to a pre-season reserve game in the rain. But things were very strained at home, and it all came to a head in the middle of one hot night in August.

Donovan first heard the shouting in his sleep; it was his mother calling him in from the street to see something on the television. When he awoke, however, although he still heard his mother's voice, she was shouting not at him but at his father. And it was not with a friendly message but with the anger of a serious grievance. He could not make out all the words, they were fast Creole, shrieked at the limits of her anger and her voice.

But the words which he did hear, and which he still clutched to him to try to understand, were uttered with a fierce explosion of her voice:

'You can't stop me! I'm going! You an' Donovan can care for yourselves . . . '

With windows wide open in the humid night the shrill wild voice carried out of the flat. It raised the windows opposite and started a knocking on the floor from upstairs. It was repeated with a rhythm, as if she were beating time—'I'm going, I'm going, I'm going'—until someone from across the back area shouted, 'For God's sake go, and shut up!' and there followed a long heavy silence which covered an angry struggle, or a low sobbing moan into a wet pillow.

With the normally sharp focus of his mind blurred by sleep Donovan did not realize how serious the situation was, and he turned over and shut his eyes again. But when he awoke next morning his mother had gone away, leaving behind a red-eyed husband and a desolate boy who could not understand what had suddenly happened to him; and since that morning life had been a hazy business in which Donovan seemed somehow detached from what was happening, as if his mind were floating outside his body.

He looked down at the scrap of fluffy white fur in his hands. Warm and trusting out of its hutch, Fluff needed him as he needed it. It was only Fluff's appearance at the front of his hutch that had enabled Donovan to recognize Keith's house at all. No one had answered his ring at the front door—it could have been the wrong house anyway—and he had climbed over several back gardens before Fluff's hutch told him he

88

had found the right house. Then, seeking refuge from the uproar caused by his climbing over flower-beds and fences, Donovan had thought Mr Chapman's shed to be a good place to hide from the shouts of the woman next door.

Donovan cradled the small guinea-pig closer, still rocking to and fro, and now flattening the whirling fur with his tears. He still couldn't understand. How could his father have sent him away? He'd been a good boy. He'd been no trouble, helping at home in the holiday, doing the cleaning while his father was at work. He'd waited up for his father—never going to bed before his father came home, however late he got in. He'd done all he could to help his father in the midst of his own suffering, and yet he'd suddenly been sent away.

He wished he could die. During those long days in the flat, pining for his mother, waiting for his father, he had felt so much alone and unwanted that his confidence in other people—even those he loved—had been slowly eaten away, as acid eats away at an ailing battery. Only his brief daily contact with his father had sustained him. But when he was sent away from his home, rejected for the second time, his trust in other people was totally destroyed. He no longer wanted to have anything to do with anyone any more, he no longer wanted to go on living.

So it was there, as he squatted, rocking and sobbing and clutching the guinea-pig, that Mr Chapman found him when he came to the shed for his bicycle.

He spoke softly to Donovan, but he was not heard, for Donovan's head was filled with the mighty sound of his own miserable cry, and there was room for nothing else.

'Why, Mam . . . why?'

9

Mr Roper was hardly out of the phone-box when the bell rang. The smell of damp concrete and old tobacco hit him again as he fought with the heavy door and grabbed at the receiver.

'039-2525 X,' he said, reading the disc with difficulty. 'Roper here.'

'Hallo, Mr Roper. This is Mr Chapman. Look, we've found him, he was in our shed. There's no need for you to go to the police. I thought you'd like to know as soon as possible.'

The delight showed on Mr Roper's face.

Not half! he thought, suddenly re-filled with sparkle and bubble. He sent a stream of praise and goodwill down the line to Mr Chapman.

'Oh good, very good; yes, that's excellent news. Oh, well done, splendid . . . '

Mr Chapman stopped him before he ran out of words. Although the boy was found, the situation didn't call for the declaration of a bank holiday.

'Yes, I'm glad he's safe too, Mr Roper,' he said. 'But he's far from all right and I want to have a long talk with you about what happened in the school today, and about what can be done to put the boy right. I'd like to make an appointment to come up to the school some time . . . '

Mr Roper stood up a little straighter and arranged his long straggly hair over his bald patch.

'Yes, yes, of course, Mr Chapman. A very good idea.

How about tomorrow morning after assembly—about half-past nine? Can you get time off at short notice?'

'I'll take it,' was Mr Chapman's terse reply. 'What about Donovan? Shall I bring him too?'

The headmaster's reply was spontaneous.

'Of course,' he said. 'Yes, bring him along.'

He was a keen 'Horse of the Year' viewer, and a sincere believer in the 'get-back-on-and-jump-the-fence' way of thinking. Donovan had to come back to school right away. He glanced out through a missing pane at Mr Henry, who looked a sorry sight in the Co-op doorway, like an officer who might be about to lose rank. The man surely couldn't make the same mistake twice. Croft was bound to be all right in Henry's class now. The headmaster turned back to the telephone again.

'Bring him with you. It will give me an excellent opportunity to meet the lad before he goes to his class.'

He didn't give Mr Chapman a chance to ask that the boy shouldn't be hit again.

'Have no fear, he'll be treated with the utmost care.'

There followed a little pause, crammed with unspoken thoughts at both ends of the line.

'Very well, then, Mr Roper. I'll see you in the morning.'

'Fine, Mr Chapman, fine. Goodbye.'

Mr Roper tried to keep a very serious face while he told the news of Donovan's safety to the forlorn Mr Henry in the doorway, although inside he was bursting with a smile of sheer relief. Mr Henry nodded his acknowledgement before he said anything. As a professional soldier he was trained to take a harsh sentence or a promotion with the same disciplined expression.

'Thank you,' he said. 'I'm very relieved. Then with your permission I'll dismiss my men and proceed home now. A few things to do . . . '

'Of course . . . '

'Good afternoon, Mr Roper.'

Mr Chapman, returning the receiver to its rest on the home-made telephone shelf in the hall, called out to Donovan:

'Well, that was Mr Roper. And it's all right. It's all over now.'

He went into the back room.

'You're safe, my lad, and we can relax and have a nice pot of tea. Now, what do you say to that?'

Donovan, sitting in the armchair by the empty summer grate, merely stared ahead. He had nothing to say to that.

The tea had only just been poured, Donovan and Mr Chapman silent in opposite armchairs drinking it, when there was a loud knocking at the front door. Expecting it to be Keith, home before his mother and without a key, Mr Chapman went to answer it. He was glad because it meant he could send Keith to find his mother and tell her Donovan was safe, while he stayed at home with the silent boy.

Both he and the caller had a surprise when he opened the door. It was Mrs Parsons, their neighbour, standing in the porch looking very much as if she had come out in the middle of doing something else. Her hair was swept up close to her head and two flattened ringlets were fastened back in pins to await their release just before she went out to her dancing club that night. She was wearing a shapeless blouse and a pair of slacks with one pink and one blue fluffy mule on her feet. She had obviously come out in a hurry over something.

She was put off her stroke at first, confronted by Mr Chapman instead of his wife, but she recovered quickly.

'Oh, it's you, Mr Chapman. Well, I want to have a word with you about this foster-boy of yours.'

'Oh yes,' said Mr Chapman.

'I know you get paid for having him, and if that's how you want to earn a few bob that's your business. But if you take the money, you've got to take the responsibility, and I'm not having him trampling all over my garden and breaking down my fence when he feels like it.'

She drew a quick breath.

'I'm not having it. I don't know what my husband's going to say. We scrimp and save to get a nice home together, and a little bit of garden, and when we turn round it's spoiled. And it's your fault, Mr Chapman. You and Mrs Chapman. You take these people on without any thought for others. It's not fair, letting them trample all over other people's property. They might not have fences where they come from, but they can't do as they like in a civilized country.'

Mr Chapman was slow to get heated in public. At the door or in the street his voice in the midst of flurry was as calm as a recorded railway announcement: it wasn't until he got indoors and started getting ratty with the family that they could tell how upset he was. On this occasion, too, he kept very cool.

'I'm sorry, Mrs Parsons, I don't quite follow. Who's been breaking down your fence?'

'Your boy,' replied the angered woman, folding her arms, determined not to be palmed off with politeness. 'He walked slow as you like through my back from next door, across Cyril's vegetable-garden and over the fence to your house. You can still see the footprints in the dirt if you don't believe me.' She patted her ringlets and refolded her arms. 'And I'm not having it. I tell you, I'm not.'

'Oh, I believe you, Mrs Parsons,' Mr Chapman replied, thinking of Cyril Parsons' pathetic vegetable-garden—two patches of cat-watered mint, an uneven row of carrots, and one of City East's finest displays of weeds.

'I'm sorry if he did any damage. He doesn't know which is our house yet, and he couldn't get in at the front.'

He looked backwards over his shoulder in an exaggerated way, like a comedian about to tell a story concerning someone behind the scenes.

'As a matter of fact, the boy is ill. Nothing serious, but he's not himself. He's very upset, and very sorry for himself. So please accept my . . . '

But he was not allowed to complete the sentence.

'Well, I'm sorry to say I told you so,' interrupted Mrs Parsons, 'but they're all the same. All they come over for is our benefits and when they get here they behave as if they own the place—they've got no respect for person or property, some of them.'

She turned to go, but she had an afterthought.

'I wouldn't mind so much if I didn't know there were people like you making a fat profit out of having them.'

Mr Chapman took a deep breath. He was angry now and it began to show. His neck went red and his eyes widened to show the whites all round.

'Well, don't you worry, woman,' he said. 'He won't bother you any more. He won't come near your garden again. And if he has broken the fence, just remember that the fence between my house and yours belongs to me. So as far as you're concerned, he can chop it up for firewood if he wants to.'

Mr Chapman shut the door in her frowning face, almost immediately ashamed of himself for losing control.

'The stupid woman,' he said to himself as he walked back to the living-room. 'Cyril's vegetable-garden!' he snorted. 'I've seen better on a damp flannel.'

'Small-minded bigots!' he exploded to Mrs Chapman when she came in ten minutes later and he told her about the finding of Donovan and their neighbour's visit.

'You don't have to look far to find them in their hundreds. They crawl out from under every stone. We've had Donovan twenty-four hours—and Keith's been in a fight, Donovan's been hit by a teacher at the school, and old mother Parsons has done her nut over Cyril's carrots. The world's getting worse instead of better. Everyone out for themselves and short shrift for anyone who doesn't fit.'

He went on like that for some time. Mrs Chapman knew better than to interrupt. He didn't often go on like that. But then he didn't often have to deal with an emotional crisis. Come to that, none of them was used to dealing with one of those.

Mrs Chapman gave them a quick and easy tea, fish-fingers and bread and butter. They all tried to behave normally, but they weren't sure what was normal any more. The mood of the meal was very much like the same meal on the previous day, just after Donovan had arrived. Donovan ate the fish-fingers on his plate without bothering to salt or pepper them or to add any sauce. Afterwards he ate two more pieces of bread and butter, ignoring the blackcurrant jam and peanut butter which were Keith's favourite spreads, and he drank one cup of tea without adding any sugar; then when he had finished he sat still on his chair, neither back as if full-up nor forward as if listening to any of the slightly forced table talk.

'Piece of cake, Donovan?' asked Mrs Chapman. He did not reply, but she put a thin slice of bright angel cake on his plate. Donovan ate it up slowly, chewing each mouthful as if he were counting the chews to ensure perfect digestion. At last he finished. Then, to everyone's surprise, he stood up and walked out of the room. The Chapmans exchanged meaningful glances. This was the first time Donovan had done anything unbidden except to put his football picture up. They sat quietly, listening for clues to his whereabouts. A few minutes later the pull of the lavatory chain, the rush of water, and the slamming of a door told them. They smirked at one another and waited for his return. But he didn't come back.

As the minutes hummed round on the electric wall clock, the three of them began looking at one another nervously, all thinking the same thing. Could he have walked down the stairs and silently out of the house? Or was he sitting moping in the spare bedroom?

Mr Chapman spoke in a light, normal voice.

'Pop upstairs, son, and see what young Donovan's up to,' he said, leaning on one elbow and trying to look casual. 'Just see he's all right and has got something to play with.'

Keith scraped his chair back to go, but just then a sudden squeak of springs from the spare room above told them that Donovan was still safe in the house, and Keith relaxed.

'Keith,' prompted Mrs Chapman. 'Go and do as Dad says—get a game out or something.'

'Oh,' moaned Keith.

'Go on.'

Keith got up slowly and opened the door.

'I don't know what to play,' he said, his resentment at the day's troubles with Donovan coming to the surface. 'I don't much fancy Snap.'

Mr Chapman aimed a friendly blow at his son's head.

'Go on, son,' he said. 'You've got so many toys. Get out your electric racing-cars or something—something to amuse him. He's had a hell of a day.'

Keith pulled a face. So had he. But they didn't seem to realize that.

Reluctantly he went out of the room and up the stairs, leaning on the wall all the way up and taking one step at a time slowly. He trod on the stair which creaked, but he didn't hear it, and he aimlessly followed the pattern of the wallpaper with his eyes. Once in his room he stretched out on his stomach on the bed and reached out lethargically for the big box which was under the cupboard on the far side. With a bit of half-hearted jiggling it came out and he then had to concentrate to lift it up over his body and onto the carpet in front of his bed. It was a real drag, having to do this.

'Racing Aces Electric Rally—all the thrills of Le Mans' it said on the lid. It was a good game, really. Keith and his dad had had some exciting hours with it kneeling on the bedroom floor, 'dicing with cramp rather than death,' Mr Chapman said, but nevertheless enjoying the challenge of doing scaled-down speeds of one and two hundred kilometres an hour for twenty or thirty laps. The drawback with the set, as Keith's dad knew well, was the time it took to set it all up. It was a fiddly business of clips and wires, and by the time it was all ready it seemed almost time to pack it away. As a consequence it was often left out for several days at a time until a combination of gathering dust and boredom led to its dismantlement.

Without any enthusiasm Keith set up a small circuit. He kept the straights fairly short and the bends simple— just one banked semi-circle at each end—so that the finished course was little more than a stretched 'O'. He set up each track with a shiny Mini and tested them simultaneously, both thumbs exerting an even pressure on the hand controllers which worked the cars. The blue and red contestants went buzzing round the circuit like two hares at a dog-track. Due to a faulty connection, or fluff, the blue car only went in fits and starts, but instead of fiddling with it, Keith kept it for himself. It was good enough for a game with Donovan. He set the red hand controller on a stool ready for the other boy, then he went to call him.

Donovan was sitting on his bed with his hands in his lap, his legs swinging and his eyes downcast staring fixedly at the rug. He did not look up as Keith went in.

'Er, Donovan, I've got my racing-cars out. D'you want to come and see them?'

Had Keith expected Donovan to jump up and say, 'Yes please, Keith,' or even, 'No thanks,' he would have been disappointed. But since he expected no answer, Keith wasn't surprised when he didn't get one.

'I've got racing Minis. Come'n see them.'

He moved over to Donovan and sat beside him on the bed.

'They're good. If you go too slow you lose the race, and if you go too fast you spin off. Just like proper motor racing. It's smart. My dad's the best. ''Slow into the bends and fast out,'' he says. Calls himself Stirling Moss. Used to be a World Champion. Stirling Moss.'

Keith looked sideways at Donovan to see if any of his acted enthusiasm was having an effect. It wasn't. Donovan's expression and posture had not changed in any way.

Keith tried a last tactic. He gripped Donovan's arm and moved off the bed.

'Come on and have a go,' he said. 'I bet you could beat me if you tried. I've got a good car for you to race.'

He gave a gentle pull and to his surprise Donovan came with him. At the door, Keith released his grip and went ahead along the landing to his own room. Without looking behind he sensed that Donovan was following him, so he said nothing until they were well inside the room and Donovan had had a chance to see the lay-out. Although small, it looked exciting: the black track with a broken white line dividing the lanes in the short straights, becoming continuous round the sweep of the bends: the glittering metal pick-up channels: and the bright Minis standing ready on the starting grid. Now that it was all set up, and seeing it all from above as he re-entered the room, Keith felt a tingle of excitement. He smiled and turned to look at Donovan's face.

Donovan might as well have been looking into an empty dustbin. He appeared to see nothing; there was not the slightest flicker of interest on his mask-like face.

'Come on,' said Keith brusquely. 'I'll show you how it works.'

He crouched down by the controllers, but Donovan remained standing. Keith looked up at the unhappy boy. His mood suddenly changed. He smiled.

'Come on, Donovan,' he said softly. 'It's easy. Come over here on the red.'

Keith held the red plastic controller up to the other boy, who looked at it suspiciously at first, but as Keith continued offering it he put his hand out and took it. His moves, it seemed, were always along the line of least resistance. When Keith thought about it, it had happened like that all day—except, of course, for the not speaking. Keith pulled Donovan towards him and got him crouching down next to him in the position for racing.

'Now, Don, all you do is press this knob with your thumb. The harder you push, the faster the car goes. But the skill is to keep it on the track. If you push too hard you'll spin your car off on one of the bends, and lose the race. Get it?'

There was no telling whether Donovan understood or not, so Keith thought the best policy was to get straight on with a race. After all, it was possible that Donovan had one of these sets at home himself, and he might turn out to be good at it. You never knew.

'Ready? Right, on your marks, get set, go!'

Keith took his car off the grid with some skill. It spurted away with a whirring of wheels and Keith felt the old thrill of the competition. He was at Brands Hatch, the sun was shining, and this was the saloon-car final. But the miniature Mini was obviously sick, and in fits and starts it began to lose power at the end of the straight. Now for the skill of the champion. Keith didn't give it full throttle in case the power returned without warning, shooting the car into the bend too fast, but by working his thumb up and down gently he slid the car into the first right-hander and took it round in a four-wheel drift. It was a smooth and skilful piece of remote-control driving, and Keith was pleased with himself. He doubted if his dad, or Stirling Moss, could have done better. So engrossed was he in getting his own car off the mark and round the first bend, that it was not until he was in the back straight that he glanced across at Donovan.

Donovan crouched, staring at the grid where his car had been. He had started some seconds after Keith, as soon as he realized the race had begun. But he had merely thrust down on the throttle with his thumb, pushing it as far as it would go, and sent the red Mini hurtling down the metre or so of track, much too fast for the corner, to go flying off in a straight line and crashing with a thud into Keith's chest of drawers.

Keith saw the red Mini lying on its back. He stopped his own car and stepped over the wires and the track to pick up the casualty. Holding it ten centimetres or so from his eyes he examined it carefully. There was a scratch on the front which might have been new, he wasn't sure, but otherwise the car seemed to have survived its crash all right. He put it back on the grid. Donovan obviously wasn't an expert racer.

'You don't want to go flat out at first,' Keith explained, 'or you'll never get round the first bend. You have to press gently to start with, till you get the feel of it, then gradually give it a bit more.'

Keith lined up his own car on the grid again and took up his position next to Donovan. Judging by his face Donovan wasn't at all interested in the game, but at least he was holding the controller in his hand and looking at his car.

'This time we'll go round together. If you keep with me you shouldn't come off,' Keith explained. 'We don't have to start racing till you've got the hang of it. All right, ready, steady, go . . . ' This was the warm-up lap at Brands before the big event.

A buzz came from the miniature cars and a slight tingling tickled the boys' palms again as the electricity flowed through the circuit. This time both cars moved off the grid more slowly, Keith's, in the inside lane, slightly ahead of Donovan's. As it took the first bend, the advantage of the lane put Keith's car further ahead, but Donovan kept the same steady pressure on his throttle and did not attempt to catch up. Keith slowed his and waited for the red car at the exit to the first bend, then he kept abreast of it down the next straight and into the next curve. Again the inside-lane advantage told and Keith went ahead once more, but again Donovan did not vary the pressure on his throttle, seeming either content to fall behind or just not interested enough to try to improve his position. His facial expression mirrored the action of his hand: his eyes were following the car he was controlling but his mind was miles away from the race.

At the end of the second bend Keith's car was a good metre ahead. Then the fluff, or the poor connection in the electric motor, played up again and like a family saloon with a cold engine, or its racing cousin with an oily plug, the blue Mini jerked to a halt, shot forward a few centimetres, then jerked to a halt again. Keith frowned. He would have to take the electric motor out and clean it. Meanwhile, he tried to clear the trouble by giving the car a burst of power. With the straight track ahead he could afford to put his thumb down for a second or so. The resistance spring in the controller squeaked as he pushed the blue knob as far as it would go, the little car responding immediately and speeding off down the black plastic track with its tail sliding from side to side as the imaginary driver fought for control at the wheel.

Donovan, just coming out of the bend, saw Keith's thumb go down and the car shoot away, and still copying Keith without thinking, he, too, gave his car full throttle. But while Keith only held it on for a second, and slid dexterously into the first bend again, Donovan just kept pushing his thumb hard down and his car, with the extra speed which the straight gave it, hurtled into the banked bend at a scale speed of two hundred kilometres an hour and carried on through the air to crash loudly into the chest of drawers again and fall with a cracking thud to the hard lino floor.

Keith threw down his hand controller and rushed over to pick the car up, but as he did so, tenderly with the tips of his fingers and thumb, the plastic body fell apart—split clean in two—and the small copper electro-magnetic motor from inside fell heavily to the floor.

'Charming!'

Keith was really upset. These cars were expensive, and he had had this one since the set was new: he had chosen the two Minis specially because his dad had had a real red one at the time. It had been a good car, this. It had contested hundreds of exciting races, and it had had its fair share of crashes—but none had been as violent, as thoughtless, and as final as this.

Without another word he threw the pieces into the Rally box.

'Oh well, that's that, i'n' it?' he said. 'That's that. Can't race with one car. We'll have to pack it in.'

He looked across at the other boy. Donovan had dropped the throttle control to the floor and was staring at where the model Mini had crashed into the chest of drawers. He remained motionless while Keith packed the whole set up, hurriedly and untidily so that it didn't fit, pressing the cardboard lid down fiercely on to the swollen box, and squeezing it with difficulty back under the bedside cupboard. Keith straightened up.

'I'm going down to watch telly,' he announced curtly. 'See you.'

With that he walked out of the room and dropped in moody thumping jumps down the stairs to the living-room.

It was some time before bed, but throughout the evening's programmes he didn't mention the breakage to anyone. He didn't forget, though, and when he eventually went to bed all his problems at school and at home—his new teacher, his broken friendships, his fight with Dave, and his ruined car—all came out in one long secret weep of self-pity. There was more than one unhappy boy in City East that night.

10

When Keith walked through the school gate alone the next morning he wasn't sure what sort of reception he was going to get. He had wondered about it on the way to school, especially (although he would never have admitted it to anyone) the sort of greeting he was likely to get from Dave and Tony. Now that they had heard Mr Roper talking about Donovan, and had joined in the search to find him, they might understand a bit more about why Keith had stuck by him. He put his hand to his face. It was still a bit puffy and tender, and he expected Dave's was the same.

No one took much notice of him at first. Unlike the first day back, everyone was now well in the swing of things, and they felt they'd never been away. The old gangs were re-established and the criss-crossing football games were already at fever pitch.

The Year Six boys had commandeered the best goals—an air-raid shelter at one side of the playground and two convenient buttresses of the Infant wall on the other. The Year Five boys, and minor Year Six players, had their pitch at right angles to the other, with one goal on the side of the school itself and the other along a section of the street railings, both distinguishable to those in the know and clearly marked by the limits of the goalkeepers' leaps.

The centre of the playground, where the two games crossed, was always the scene of fierce soccer activity and only the bravest non-player would venture there. A few of the big girls sometimes did, just to get in the way, but by and large it was a disaster area to be avoided like Hyde Park Corner in the rush-hour.

Keith watched two sets of boys tackling for the possession of a pair of plastic footballs not three metres apart. One ball was being pounded by Year Fives, the other, slightly more skilfully, by Year Six boys and hopeful members of the school team. Somehow they avoided one another, and suddenly, while the Year Fives remained in the centre hacking away at their ball, the other group took off after a tall Year Six striker who made a streak for the Infant wall goal and scored easily.

The goal scorer turned swiftly and ran fast in a straight line to the centre spot, his arms raised stiffly in a proud gesture of triumph. The rest of his team jumped up and down in delight—while the other side changed goalies for the third time. That was six nil.

While they were sorting themselves out for the centre, still hampered by occasional interference from the third-year game, Joseph Rooks (whose ball it was) saw Keith standing watching. Keith was tall and quite useful, and his side certainly needed strengthening. A quick transfer deal was arranged on the touchline.

'Wanna game, Chapman?'

'Don't mind.'

'Right. On ours.'

The captain dutifully informed the other side, who had no skipper.

''Ere you lot—Chapman's on our side!'

The news was greeted with a few derisory shouts and a clear sarcastic cry of 'Good luck!' But just as the centre was about to be taken, a long shrill whistle blew: Mrs Pressnose had brought the game to a temporary halt, and school to another beginning.

'Same teams at playtime?' was the shout.

'Same teams.'

'Right. See you.'

The losers' captain collected his ball while the general movement and disorder of the playground was magically transformed into twelve lines of more or less still and silent children.

Keith took his place in the class line on his own. He suddenly felt very lonely. He tried not to look as if he was looking out for Dave and Tony: but he was, and he was disappointed to see them pointedly ignoring him two or three places nearer the front. It looked as if the two of them still hated his guts. It was going to be another rotten day, with both of them doing their best to make his life a misery. When Joseph Rooks called across to Keith they both turned round and took in every word.

'Don't forget playtime, Chapman—you're on our side.'

Keith had seen Dave and Tony look round, and he nodded back to Rooks with as little movement of his head as he could manage. Dave had seen it, however.

'We're not good enough for Chapman,' he said in a loud voice. 'He's crawling with them Year Six. That's ten goals to the other side for a start!'

Tony gave a loud, snorting giggle and thumped Dave in appreciation of his wit. Then Mrs Pressnose walked towards their line and everyone turned to face the front as the whistle was blown again.

'Now, we're all going to lead in quietly,' Mrs Pressnose shouted above the odd whisper and murmur. 'Let's start the day off as we mean it to go on.'

Keith stared up at the blue sky and the towering turrets of Transport Avenue School.

No chance, he thought bitterly. No chance.

Donovan was at last introduced to Mr Roper by Mr Chapman, up on the platform outside the headmaster's room. But despite an encouraging and benign look on the headmaster's face—a bit forced like a television quizmaster—the boy said nothing. Mr Roper took him to his classroom, holding his hand and chatting desperately in his high nasal voice all the way across the hall. At the classroom door he gave Donovan—and a meaningful look—to Mr Henry.

'Here he is, Mr Henry. Our lad is back again, ready for a good day's work. He may not have much to say, but I expect he can put plenty down on paper.'

A huge wink behind the boy's head was seen by every child in the class. Then, as Donovan was led gently to his desk by Mr Henry, quiet and fussy, Mr Roper returned to the boy's foster-father.

Mr Chapman looked smart in his Crimplene blazer and grey slacks.

'I won't beat about the bush, Mr Roper. My wife and I are very upset about what happened in school yesterday . . .'

The headmaster opened his mouth to apologize.

'. . . but after a long talk last night we decided to let it go there. We won't do much good by getting a teacher into trouble. But I want your word, Mr Roper, that nothing of the sort will ever happen again.'

Mr Roper shut his mouth again, then quickly re-opened it to reassure the man. Mr Chapman went on.

'What really worries us, though, is this dumbness. Now, we know it isn't normal for the boy. The Health Department gave him a clean bill of health, there was no mention of a talking problem. So the question arises, what's the matter with him? And what can we do about it?'

Mr Roper sat back and pressed his fingertips together, more relaxed now that he and Henry had been let off the hook.

'It's not an easy matter, Mr Chapman,' he began

slowly, 'and I must say I'm no expert on the subject. But you know, this dumbness hasn't been going on for very long, and he could quite easily begin speaking again as suddenly as he stopped.'

Mr Chapman listened intently, giving the headmaster a fair hearing.

'We both know that his mother has gone abroad—quite suddenly by all accounts. Your wife also told me that the lad had to be forced into the car by his father to be brought to you . . .'

Mr Chapman nodded, and the headmaster casually began unbending a paper-clip between his fingers.

'So it doesn't need a detective to tell us that he didn't want to come. No reflection on you or your good wife, but for some reason he did not want to come.' He paused. 'Understandable, of course. He probably wants his mum and dad . . .'

Mr Chapman nodded again. He quite agreed. It was only surprising that Donovan hadn't run off in an attempt to get home.

'Now in the light of all that, can we really wonder at the unfortunate lad's attitude? He has decided to punish the world by not talking to it. Yes?'

'Yes . . .' Mr Chapman began.

'Think about it, Mr Chapman. It's not very hard to understand what might be happening in the boy's head, is it? He's a lonely lad who is suddenly made to feel unwanted by his parents. One minute everyone's at home and all's well: the next, his mother goes away, and before he knows what's hit him the lad is sent off by his father. How would I feel, how would you feel, in such a situation? Rejected. Spurned. Unwanted. Quite naturally, he doesn't want to have anything to do with anyone. Now don't you think that if *you* can make him feel really at home with your family, and *we* can put matters right here at school, there might be a good chance he'll start speaking normally again before long?'

Mr Chapman nodded once more, finally this time. 'I see,' he said. He thought for a few moments while Mr Roper started unbending another paper-clip. 'That's very interesting.' There certainly seemed to be something in what the headmaster had said. It seemed to make sense.

'Anyway, Mr Chapman, we'll give it a couple of days, put our thinking-caps on, and see how things go. How does that strike you?'

He stood up, hoping that the other would too. He did.

'Yes, that seems all right for a start,' Mr Chapman agreed. 'We must keep in touch, and above all, not let the situation get out of hand again . . . I definitely don't want any more of that hitting business . . . '

Mr Roper put on his sincerest smile.

'I give you my word, Mr Chapman. My word.'

No one ever makes an entrance into a classroom quite like a boy in trouble. Whether he is proud of himself, and swaggers in with a grin, or ashamed of himself, and creeps in hoping no one is looking, he can be sure of being followed by a full house of eyes. This was Mr Henry's experience.

So it was with Donovan. Although he fitted into neither category he was a school celebrity now and he commanded the complete attention of the class as he was escorted to his seat. Perhaps the most intent observer was Keith, who followed his foster-brother closely with his eyes, searching for some small sign of recognition. But there was none. Donovan kept his eyes on the floor until he had sat down, then he silently surveyed the objects which had been placed on his desk before school.

Mr Henry was no fool. He did not want to be disobeyed, even in a good cause, and to avoid any danger of this happening he made sure that anything Donovan might need that morning was already set out. In the groove there were two newly sharpened pencils, and lying alongside them a new metric ruler. A rough work-book sat squarely in the middle of the desk, flanked on one side by a graded reading-book, *Careful Hans*, and on the other by a copy of *New English Exercises for Juniors*. A small white rubber on the top of the exercise-book completed the kit.

'Here you are, Donovan,' said Mr Henry kindly. 'Everything you'll need this morning.'

There was a muted snigger from somewhere at the back of the class which Mr Henry chose to ignore.

'If you need anything else just put your hand up and I'll come and help you. Do you understand?'

Mr Henry smiled at him encouragingly, and with a little embarrassment. After all, he had slapped the boy's face hard yesterday. 'You're not to worry about anything, Croft, is that clear? Remember, I'm here to help you.' Without warning he looked round at the inquisitive class. They were sitting with their mouths open, surprised at seeing this side of their teacher's nature. He was going soft. Mr Henry was quick to sense the atmosphere.

'This isn't a peep-show,' he said forcefully, warning the rest that he wasn't going soft on everyone. 'Get on with your work, all of you. And woe betide anyone who hasn't done twenty by playtime.'

The teacher opened Donovan's *New English Exercises for Juniors* and showed him the exercise he was to do.

'Best writing,' he said, a little more sternly for the sake of the others, 'and think about what you're doing.'

Mr Henry walked back to his desk and pretended to add his register column. It had all been completed before Donovan arrived, by a different method in which the children just reported any vacant desks, but it gave him something to do. While moving his pencil up the tall column he kept flicking his eyes under lowered lids in Donovan's direction. He was keen to see if the boy attempted to do any work.

He was a little surprised to see that he did. Picking up his pencil in his right hand and lowering his head to within ten centimetres of the paper, Donovan started on the exercise. With as little movement of his head as he could manage, and with his left arm protecting his work from prying eyes, he looked backwards and forwards from English book to rough work-book and in backward-slanting handwriting he 'completed the sentences' as requested.

'1. A pilot . . . an aeroplane. (drives, glides, flies)
2. A hunter . . . a trap. (catches, sets, springs) . . . '

Sitting behind him, Keith worked steadily through the same exercise. He quite enjoyed it. It was straightforward, not much brain-work required, a good way of passing the time to playtime. It was all part of growing older and growing up, he thought, leaving behind the poetry writing and stories of Miss Davis's class for this other sort of English.

The warm September morning drifted in on the dust and settled on the bent heads of the silent children. An occasional pencil fell woodenly to the floor, a foot scraped here and there, and Mr Henry's blakeyed heels clicked slowly up and down the aisles as he looked at their work without seeing it.

'I'll see when I mark it,' was all he said when children asked if an answer was right or wrong.

So the dozy morning drifted on.

At last the playtime bell went, the pencils, as usual, were put prematurely down, and the customary caution was given.

'That's a signal to me,' said Mr Henry, raising his voice

then dropping it, 'not you. Remember that next time. Now, put your books in a neat pile, open, on my desk— and lead out quickly and quietly file by file.'

Straight, innocent faces above tripping feet and digging elbows made a pushing race to the door look orderly, and by the time the teacher had looked up from tidying his pile of books, the room was clear. Even Donovan Croft had made his exit with the rest.

Mr Henry extracted Donovan's book from the large folded-over pile. It was very neat, and the boy had worked reasonably quickly. He had got to number sixteen out of the total of twenty. Not bad. But it was number twelve which caught the teacher's eye. Donovan had completed the sentence, but he had done so without using any of the words given.

'A house is where people . . . ' was completed not with 'live', 'work', or 'play', from which Donovan should have chosen, but with a word out of Donovan's head—'love'.

Mr Henry looked at it for a moment, frowning. Then he automatically reached for his red ballpoint and put a long 'S' down through the word—'S' for 'spelling mistake'.

The school burst out into the bright sunshine like water through a dam, rushing and leaping outwards and finally finding its own various levels in different games all over the playground. Some of the games, like the football, were highly organized; others were very simple, consisting of little more than shoving someone in the back and running away. Some games involved many children, others— especially the girls'—involved just ones and twos.

Keith walked out with Donovan and stood at the bottom of the steps, squinting in the sun. It was too nice a day to be unhappy, but the weather pays little regard to anyone's feelings. Keith really hoped Joseph Rooks and the team would have found someone else to play in their game. It would help not to give Dave and Tony a reason for sniping at him. Perhaps he could get a game with the boys in his own class instead, and maybe play well on Dave's and Tony's side. That would help a lot. But these were daydreams, and quite unrealistic.

A sudden shouting outpouring of Year Six boys pushed Keith and Donovan down the steps and onto the asphalt pitch. The teams were coming out, shouting their own welcome in the absence of a huge crowd.

'We are the champions!'

A group of the boys who hoped to play for the school, to share the privilege of a ride in Sir's car on Saturday mornings, shouted their own ambitious chant to the tune of 'Deck the Halls'.

'Transport is the pride of Europe, tra-la-la, la-la, la-la!'

'We are the champions!'

'Cobblers!'

So, in an atmosphere of joyful unrestrained shouting, theirs for the taking three times a day, the teams lined up.

Just before they kicked off, by mutual consent instead of by whistle, Joseph Rooks spotted Keith.

'Come on, Chapman. You're on our side. Midfield schemer.'

'All right. I know,' said Keith, moving forward reluctantly.

'Come on, then.'

Keith turned to Donovan, who was leaning against the wall watching the high arching flight of the Year Five's ball.

'I'm in this game. I've got to go. I'll see you when the whistle goes.'

Not sure about leaving the other boy, and unhappy about what Dave and Tony would say when they saw him playing, Keith walked over behind Joseph Rooks and waited for the start. A goal had just been scored in the other game so there were two kick-offs to be taken together, the games at right angles to one another. It didn't seem to matter. Nobody in one game really saw the other: except, on this occasion, Dave, Tony, and Keith.

The teams in Keith's game had decided to start level, nil–nil, and Joseph Rooks was taking the centre. He glanced round to ensure that his men were all in position, then he shouted, 'They're off!' and rolled the ball sideways to the inside-right, Jaspal, a small Asian boy in a pale blue turban. As the opposing team charged in, Jaspal back-kicked neatly to Keith and ran out to the right wing, calling for the return ball in a fast stream of words.

Keith put his foot on the ball to steady it and took a quick look round. He wasn't sure who was on his side. It was easy for City East: at least they all wore the same colour shirts. Here in the playground your own team grew on you during the course of a game, but at the beginning you had to assume that those running away from you were on your side, and those coming towards you were the opposition—while those doing something else were in a different game altogether. Keith saw three boys converging on him at speed, so trying to judge the direction and distance accurately he kicked the return ball to Jaspal on the wing.

The opposing defence, sated with goals in the game before school, had pushed up well into Keith's half, each member looking for a chance to do some scoring himself. As a result they were thin at the back, and the small winger, fast and skilful, took the ball outside a group of girls playing hopscotch and, leaning back, was able to send a high ball across from the corner post into a ruck of jostling players in the goal mouth.

By now, seeing their mistake in pushing forward too

soon, the whole of the defence scurried back to scramble the ball away, and Keith's team's attack ran up, hoping for a lucky header and an early goal.

It was a good cross. Like most light plastic balls it picked up height quickly and it hung in the air tantalizingly just short of the near post. The goalkeeper, an athletic boy in a vest and jeans, was pleased to get some action for a change and positioned himself well for what should have been a confident two-handed catch above his head. But the plastic ball, instead of completing its arch, dropped suddenly short and prevented the goalkeeper from catching the ball cleanly. The best he could do was fist it out.

Close games of football are won as much on luck as on skill, and even Keith was able to cash in on a whim of chance. The ball glanced off the goalkeeper's fist, bounced over a cluster of heads, and dropped beautifully down towards Keith's right foot. He was perfectly positioned for a shot at goal. Instinctively he made the decision to hit it first time. Any fiddling about would give the whole lot time to turn and pounce on him.

Nine times out of ten first-time volleys from that position, even in a top-class game, go soaring over the grandstand to great shouts of derision from the crowd. But this must have been a tenth time, for Keith caught it just right on his plimsolled instep, and with an awkward dipping spin the orange ball shot through a gap in the turning legs and bounced hard and decisively against the wall.

'Goal!' came a throaty roar from a dozen boys.

'Offside!' complained a couple of peeved defenders, giving the traditional response. No one took any notice, however, and the boys turned back to re-start the game, some of them running and whooping, the others walking and moaning. It was easy to tell who was who now.

Keith walked back slowly and proudly. Scoring that

goal was the best thing that had happened to him in two days. It was one bright, proud moment that he could savour among the misery of the rest. He tried to keep a straight face as the others congratulated him, but it was difficult not to allow a faint smile of satisfaction from twitching at the corners of his mouth.

'Good goal, Chapman!'

'Nice one, son!'

Keith clapped his hands purposefully like a professional to say 'Keep it up'. Then he lined up behind his forwards for the centre.

'Lucky old goal that!' said a familiar voice just behind him.

'Couldn't have missed,' agreed another, with a snorting giggle.

Keith didn't have to turn round to know who was behind him. Dave and Tony had seen him score, and it seemed to have hurt them as much as if it had been scored against their own side.

'Bloody lucky.'

Keith kept facing front, willing the other team to kick off quickly so that he could run away and get involved in the game, but they were rearranging their defence with hoarse shouts and they weren't quite ready.

Luck next fell at Dave's feet. The ball from his own game came skidding over the asphalt with little pattering bounces and ran across in front of him. It was a well-meant pass and he was expected to do something constructive with it. But it seemed to him to be a heaven-sent opportunity to do something else. As instinctively as Keith had taken his shot at goal, Dave swung at the ball in front of him and drove it with all the aggression he could muster in Keith's direction. It scorched through the air with a soft swish, sounding like an Agincourt arrow. Like Keith's shot it was good and accurate. Like Keith's shot it sped with great force to its target, and like Keith's shot it landed with a loud crack—but smacking with a painful slap into the back of Keith's neck.

The pain shot through his head, his eyes filled with water, and he tasted blood in his mouth.

'Ow!' he yelled, swinging round to face the direction the ball had come from, his head bowed and both hands clutching the back of his neck.

Dave was standing there, smiling.

'Sorry, Chapman,' he said. 'Accident.'

Tony giggled.

Keith's first reaction was to go for Dave and lay one on his stupid nose. But as he took a half step forward, both Dave and Tony squared up a bit, their fists clenched at their sides, broad grins on their faces, ready and waiting for a fight.

Keith's head was spinning, and there was a high-pitched whining in his ears. The back of his neck was red and hot and stinging. He knew what his dad meant when he said that expensive professional balls might hurt, but the cheap plastic imitations hurt more.

Keith felt rotten: he didn't want to play football any more, and he didn't want to fight Dave and Tony. His moment of triumph and pleasure had been painfully brief. Without a word he walked away from the middle of the playground like a man being replaced after injury by a substitute, his hand still held to the back of his bent head.

He walked away without hearing the shouts of 'Come on, Chapman', 'Don't be a baby', 'You're all right'. He walked over to the school steps and stood leaning against the wall next to someone he felt happier with.

'Rotten lot,' he said, and in a few well-chosen words he found himself telling his troubles to Donovan Croft.

11

The next three weeks were difficult ones for everyone from Donovan's remotest contact, Mr Roper, to his closest, Keith—although even the headmaster managed to put his head round Mr Henry's door once a day and make an oblique reference to Donovan's progress.

'Any change in the . . . situation?' he would ask, too obscure even for Mr Henry once or twice when the teacher's mind was elsewhere. But the answer was always much the same: 'No, working well but still in a world of his own.'

Donovan did work well, probably because there was nothing to distract him. Once the novelty of having a mute in the class wore off, nobody bothered to have anything to do with him, not to talk to him, to pass him secret messages, nor even to kick him or to jump on his back. He was left well alone. So there was no temptation to look at anything except what was put before him.

Donovan's view of the world was through an inferior lens which could only focus on what was immediate and dead ahead. The rest was blurred and distorted, the total effect like the reflection in the back of a spoon. He saw only what was about to happen next, at close quarters, now; his view was very limited. This could be seen by his attitude to food, at school dinners and at home. He only ate what was in front of him, he never went up for seconds at school, or put out a hand for more at home. Hunger or bodily need didn't seem to be important: he merely continued to eat out of habit. It seemed that now that his mother was gone, and his father had sent him away, his world had collapsed about his head. His will to live was weak, and in common with many old people at the end of a full life, he would have silently faded away but for the strangers around him.

Jollying along had no chance of working in such a case. Mr Chapman often talked to the boys about various things, commenting on items in the newspaper, on programmes on the television, or asking them what-have-you-been-doing-at-school questions: a hundred and one contrived attempts to stimulate conversation. But they could never succeed.

One night in Donovan's bedroom Ted Chapman had thought he was about to make the breakthrough. As he tucked the boy in and patted his head he mentioned the photograph of the Park Lane team which still dominated the room.

'Not a bad old lot,' he said with a chuckle. 'But not a patch on City East. The team of the future, City East.' He laughed. 'The remote future, some say.'

Donovan looked up at him with eyes open a fraction wider than he had seen them before. Mr Chapman jumped fast on this fleeting opportunity.

'Your team is it? Park Lane?'

There was a long silence, Donovan looking up at the smiling man.

'Are they good? Worth supporting?'

Mr Chapman felt sure, and just for a moment very sure, that Donovan was about to nod, merely a fractional movement of the head, but a nod, a communication. He looked at the boy and smiled encouragement, his eyebrows raised, his arms folded in a relaxed pose. He held it as long as he could. But the moment passed, and with a minute movement of a muscle Donovan's face resumed its customary closed look. Mr Chapman said goodnight softly and went out of the room, disappointed.

When he got downstairs he told his wife about his disappointment. 'I must have imagined it,' he said. 'There was no reaction at all really. He even seems past crying now.'

Mrs Chapman said nothing at first but after a bit of thought at the sink, her eyes staring out of the window while her hands rubbed vigorously under the hot suds, she suddenly said, 'You know, Ted, the one thing we haven't done is talk to him . . .'

Mr Chapman spluttered into his teacup. 'Stone the crows!' he said. 'What the dickens do you think I've been doing every night this week? I've been rabbiting on like "News at Ten" . . .'

'No, you don't understand,' Mrs Chapman placated him. 'You've been very good. What I mean is, no one has tried to talk to him about his mother. We've all avoided talking about her, as if she was dead. I was just thinking it might help if I tried to explain it all to him . . . sort of brought it out into the open and got him to see it's not going to last for ever.'

Mr Chapman nodded thoughtfully.

'It's too late now. I'll have a word with him in the morning,' Mrs Chapman went on, rinsing the lather off her hands and drying them, red and steaming, on the roller towel. 'It might help—and we've got nothing to lose.'

It was clear to Mr Chapman that her mind was made up. She was quite right, he thought. Nothing could make matters worse.

'I'll have a word with him out here on his own, after breakfast while I'm washing up.'

Mrs Chapman favoured the kitchen, and washing-up time, for doing important bits of family business. There were several reasons for this. It was a naturally busy area where people met casually, without fuss—and there was a lot to be said for catching people unawares. It was a place where people were usually standing up—and she found it easier to do important or awkward things when she was on her feet. And she could conduct the business from the sink with her back to the others. (She felt it was easier if her eyes didn't meet theirs when she was saying something personal or critical.) So far, events had proved her right. On many occasions she had turned the tide of family affairs with the aid of a bowl of washing-up water in the kitchen.

The next morning when Donovan carried out his used cereal bowl, holding it out in front of him in both hands like Oliver Twist, Mrs Chapman was waiting at the sink. She turned and took the bowl from him with a brisk, 'Thanks, Donovan.' She submerged it quickly and began to rub it vigorously, almost in one movement. As she rubbed, she spoke.

'By the way, Donovan, I wanted a little word with you.' She turned and smiled at him for a moment before continuing. 'It's about your mother.'

Donovan's eyes, vacantly staring at the rainbow bubbles sliding off the dishes in the rack, looked up at the back of Mrs Chapman's head. It was a simple, almost reflex, action. There was no change in focus; his eyes simply took in a new field of vision like a remote-controlled camera, and there was no indication that the movement of his head hadn't been part of some computerized move.

'You must remember, Donovan, that she hasn't gone for ever,' the busy woman went on. 'She's only gone home to look after your grandad for a bit. As soon as he's better she'll be back here like one o'clock, you mark my words.'

Donovan stood still, his arms in their usual limp

position by his sides, his eyes still staring up at Mrs Chapman.

'It won't be for long, so try and cheer up. She'll be home before you know it, and you'll wonder what all the fuss was about.'

There wasn't a sound of any sort from behind her, so she went on: 'You know your dad can't keep you, don't you? He works such long hours: and it isn't good for a boy to be on his own in a house all that time. And what about if anything went wrong—if a fire broke out or something? You might be hurt, and your dad wouldn't have a leg to stand on with the authorities. So don't go thinking no one wants you, Donovan. It's only a sensible arrangement that's been done for the best: for the time being. That's why you're here, and that's why we want you . . . '

With a swift swirl of the bowl she sent the water gurgling down the sink and she wiped the clinging suds away with the dishcloth. Then she turned to see what effect her words had had on the silent boy.

But to her surprise he wasn't there any more, and from way up the hall she heard the slow, heavy closing of the front door as Donovan went to school. She sighed. It didn't always pay to have your back to someone when you had something personal to say.

There were many such disappointments for the Chapmans; but at school Mr Henry expected little. He was careful to put no undue pressure on the boy. It became clear that Donovan would obey any simple straightforward instruction which did not involve speaking, so it was easy to avoid a battle of wills like before by keeping him occupied with simple straightforward work. All Mr Henry wanted was a quiet life.

Donovan was best at the sort of work which involved writing quietly at his desk. When Mr Henry taught from the blackboard, Donovan took scant notice, preferring to sit with his eyes on his own desk top, but when he was given a book or a work-card he would concentrate for fifteen or thirty minutes at a time. During games and PE lessons he was allowed to stay behind in the classroom, reading or staring ahead. He was put in one football team-game in the first week, but he stood rooted to the spot and became a hazard to himself and to both sides, and like a wreck in a busy channel he had to be removed. In art lessons, which were conducted at individual desks from small black tins of water-colours, Donovan merely covered the paper with a wash of khaki, making no attempt to depict any object, real or imagined. He scrubbed his brush round in scratchy circles in the manner of a four-year-old, and Mr Henry had to rescue the picture before the metal bristle-holder went right through the paper. Nevertheless, the painting was given a place on the wall.

'An Abstract Design—by Donovan Croft.'

'Croft's crap,' as one boy unkindly described it.

Most of the children ignored Donovan altogether. In his first two or three days at school there were many who thought they would be the ones to get him to speak. Some told him jokes, others told him their secrets; two or three of the girls mothered him—got his books, left a sweet on his desk, took him into dinner; and several boys tried to anger him into speech or some other action.

'Can't talk—got no brains.'

'Dumb Donovan!'

'Dumb, dumb, 'cept 'is bum!'

But after a day or so, being greeted with the reaction of a human wall—total disregard—they gave up. There was no fun in it. They found that even Keith refused to be drawn into more trouble on Donovan's account, usually by pretending not to hear, and there were easier ways of being amused. So Donovan and Keith were forgotten.

At home, Mrs Chapman found him to be co-operative in most matters so long as he had an easy course of action and he was not required to speak. He washed himself, dressed himself, covered up his own bed in the mornings, but he would ask for nothing, by word or by gesture.

One night, as an experiment, Mrs Chapman gave drying-up towels to the two boys at the end of tea. She nodded to Keith and winked at Mr Chapman.

'Dad's got some paper-work to do,' she said. 'Could you boys give me a hand with the washing-up?'

Keith did his best to sound enthusiastic as he replied, 'Yes' to his mother. He got up and led the way into the kitchen. Then he turned to rope Donovan in.

'Come on, Don, no way out of it . . . I'll wash and you wipe.'

Donovan followed Keith to the sink, and when the plates had been given a none-too-thorough dip and brush in the hot water, Donovan took them out of the rack and dried them with a long series of slow circular strokes.

That was the beginning of a little routine into which Donovan fell easily, while Keith slipped away whenever he got the chance—often to a sudden and most urgent call to the lavatory. Donovan reported for duty at the kitchen sink every night from then on without being asked, and in his measured manner, staring intently at each plate as if it were the only one in the world, he completed his task. Whoever was at the sink with him would talk and joke as the crockery was passed from one to the other, but there was never the glimmer of a reply from Donovan. Even when a plate was dropped in being passed from Mr Chapman's slippery fingers to Donovan's, falling with a loud crash on the kitchen floor, there was no reaction from

Donovan, although Mr Chapman gave a shout of surprise and felt foolish.

There was one routine which Donovan established for himself, the nearest he got to asking to do something. After school, as soon as he got in, he went through to the hutch in the garden and fed Fluff. He had a soft spot for Fluff: he could think his troubles at him, and the small pink eyes would listen without a blink. First, while the trembling guinea-pig hid in its dark sleeping compartment, Donovan spread fresh straw, filled the water hopper and tipped a palmful of rabbit pellets and chopped carrot into the feeding-dish. Then, before leaving the small animal to explore its new mixture of food, he lifted it out of the hutch and cradled it in his warm hands, running his fingers and thumbs through the smooth whirls of white fur, thinking his private thoughts. He stood like that, as still and as silent as the guinea-pig in his palms, until a noise or a voice from the house broke the mood. It was ten minutes out of the day when he seemed to be content, doing something he appeared to like, and on a very simple level making some communication with another living creature.

In the evenings they would all sit round and watch the television. It gave everyone something to look at and it provided an excuse not to talk when silence was preferred; no games or other activities had to be organized and it gave all the Chapmans a chance to forget their problem for a while.

No one asked Keith out to play any more so he didn't go. He wasn't too keen on reading, and he had learned not to waste time trying to interest Donovan in his toys. So with the others he sat and watched the box.

On the second Saturday night, 'Match of the Day' featured Park Lane's home game with Liverpool, traditionally a tough noisy match with few goals but plenty of action. In the Chapmans' living-room the family sat round to see the recording. To Keith every Saturday night in the season included television football and a bar of chocolate, the weekly explosion of packed and noisy top matches providing a sharp contrast to his experience of the empty terraces of City East. To Donovan the television viewing of the game was the novelty. Back at home—in the good old days for which he yearned—he had been expected to be in bed before television football came on; and the Sunday afternoon game on the other channel was never seen because he was at Sunday School. The difference between him and Keith was that while Keith watched the television highlights, Donovan had often stood through the whole ninety minutes, the good games with the bad games, from the middle of a swaying crowd up behind one of the goals. With his dad. With his sorely missed dad.

Keith and his father, knowing Donovan's interest in the Park Lane team, exchanged meaningful glances when the game was announced, each hoping that this might give the boy some pleasure, raise a smile.

Sadly, it was not to be. The programme only made matters worse. The cameras switched several times to a part of the ground where Donovan stood, and the microphones picked up the familiar chants. Donovan sat and stared, his thoughts submerged deep beneath the surface. He did not move for the full forty minutes. Watching the game, seeing the familiar Park Lane ground, was unbearably sad, like seeing a happy house from which you've moved. A small treat, aimed to please, it had driven Donovan deeper within himself as he thought of those ordinary happy days.

· Park Lane won well, but that made no difference. The others in the room looked to see Donovan's reaction at the end of the game, expecting perhaps a brief look of pleasure, or of satisfaction. Donovan saw them watching him through the blurred lenses of his misery. From an already low level his spirit had plummeted further and a desperately keen sense of yearning filled his body.

Seeing the boy, Mrs Chapman thought she understood. The television had been upsetting for him, she knew that now. And no one had been sharp enough to realize it. Donovan could only sit and let it hurt, silent, dejected; and with the others she went to bed depressed with the continuing lack of progress.

So the days had their ups and downs. On the Monday after the television football disappointment, a letter came with a North London postmark. It was addressed to Mrs Chapman, and she guessed immediately what it was. Donovan's fostering was voluntary—Mr Croft agreed with it and there had had to be no court hearing—so the cost was borne by him. This must be the money, she thought.

The money was certainly there, a postal order to cover the first two weeks, and a very short note to go with it. But there was also an envelope addressed to Donovan. Feeling pleased, Mrs Chapman took it up to him in his room when she went to call him. Retreating outside the door she heard the envelope being torn open, and then she tiptoed away.

Breakfast was eaten as usual. Keith was late and in a tearing hurry, but he insisted on having two bowls of milk-swamped cornflakes. Donovan ate one, disregarded the marmalade and toast, and stood waiting by the front door for Keith. Mrs Chapman, paying particular attention, noticed that his behaviour was very little different from that of any other morning. When Keith had thumped up and down the stairs for the third time, the two boys left the house for school, as usual.

An hour later, Mrs Chapman went up to make the beds.

Keith's room, true to form, looked as if the police had just turned it over in a search for a micro-film: Donovan's looked uninhabited except for a slightly rumpled bed and a screwed-up ball of paper in the grate. As Mrs Chapman picked up the paper it fell into two, and she saw that it was an envelope and a single sheet of writing-paper— Donovan's letter from his dad.

The temptation to smooth out the paper and read the letter was very strong: it had obviously upset Donovan further, even if he hadn't shown it on his face, or it would now have been safe in his pocket or his drawer instead of lying discarded in the grate. It was all very strange. She didn't pretend to understand what was going on in the boy's mind.

As she dusted along the chest of drawers she began to wonder whether the letter might hold some clue to the mystery. It might explain Donovan's strange behaviour. If it did, she ought to know. On the other hand, she thought, it had been clearly addressed to Donovan and she ought not to read it without his permission.

She left the crumpled paper on Donovan's mantelpiece and went into her own room to make the big bed. She turned the matter over in her mind as she worked. It was a delicate problem: there was much to be gained by reading the letter, but it would amount to a betrayal of confidence if she did so. She would be justified in reading it, but she ought not to.

She was halfway through making the bed when she suddenly dropped the sheet and walked quickly into Donovan's room. He couldn't give his permission even if she asked him; he wouldn't speak and he wouldn't nod; and the whole family was being affected by his behaviour. Any clue would be valuable if it led to getting Donovan talking again. The end justified the means.

She smoothed the letter out on the bed and read it.

129

'Hallo D,

This is your daddy writing. I've been writing to you all week but been late at work. I had to work Sundays too on rush jobs so I have not seen you as hoped. But be grown up about it, like I was at your age. I hope you're being good till we hear from your mammy and get you back home. Please Lord it will not be long. I am sorry you had to go but I can't look after you. I got two hours off Saturday and saw the old team. They beat Liverpool like they should. Be good. See you soon.

Your loving
daddy.'

Mrs Chapman sat on the edge of the bed, thinking. There was no clue there to Donovan's peculiar behaviour. His father seemed a nice ordinary sort of man—hardworking and loving. Admittedly, she had wondered if he might have visited on one of the weekends, but the letter explained how busy he was at work. There was absolutely no suggestion of any trouble, or unhappiness, that she hadn't already been told about: no reason whatever for Donovan's chosen silence.

Her first reaction was to write to Mr Croft. Donovan was his son and he ought to know about his dumbness. It might have happened before and he could perhaps shed some light on the problem. But as she gave it more thought she slowly changed her mind. The man was in no position to take the boy back, and to know how unhappy the boy was would only make him fret needlessly. No, she wouldn't write. Of course, it would be different if the man should happen to come to the house. If he chose to visit them, out of the blue, she could tell him about their problem; and it would be a great help. A visit from Donovan's dad would be bound to remove some of Donovan's worries.

Perhaps next weekend. A visit on Saturday or Sunday would make all the difference.

But the week went by, and the following weekend, and there was no sign of Mr Croft. From what he'd written in the letter, perhaps this was how it had been for him at some time as a boy; perhaps he thought it better not to come and then have to go away, parting from Donovan again.

The next week was much as the two that had gone before. There was no change in Donovan's attitude or his behaviour—he plodded along at school, he existed at home, he got up, went to school, came home, watched television, and went to bed. And in all that time he still managed to have no direct communication with anyone, not even with Keith.

Keith shared the weight of Donovan's burden more than anyone. The others were kind and well-meaning, but it was *his* friendships which Donovan's coming had mucked up, not his parents' nor his teachers'. It was Keith who shared his toys; it was Keith who was left to look after Donovan for the bulk of the time when they were not in class or at the meal table. It was Keith who found himself not doing the things which Donovan couldn't do also— the playground football and the school clubs. It was Keith who was aware of Donovan and his problem when the others could switch off: Mr Chapman to his factory, Mrs Chapman to her housework, Mr Henry to his classwork, Mr Roper to his headship. It was Keith who sat behind, walked beside, and slept next door to the silent, disturbed boy. It was Keith who was giving and giving out all the time.

Fortunately, Mrs Chapman was clever enough to see some of this. On the third Monday she telephoned Mr Roper just before school began. She came straight to the point.

'I'm sorry to bother you, Mr Roper,' she said, 'but, you know, we've not seen any difference in Donovan at home—we hoped he'd be talking by now—and I'm wondering if you've seen any improvement in him at school?'

Mr Roper's routine checks on Donovan, a little less frequent now, had kept him in some touch with the boy. Of late there had been many problems in the school, and this was one which he had temporarily shelved. But he knew there had been no advance, and he could see clearly that something would have to be done.

'Well, we're very pleased with his written work, Mrs Chapman; his arithmetic and English are both very fair; but I'm afraid we've seen no improvement either in the speech problem. As a matter of fact, I did want a word with you . . . '

'Yes?'

'I want him to be seen by a doctor. I want to refer him, as we say, but I never like making any move to have children seen by school doctors without the approval of the parents . . . '

'I see . . . '

' . . . even when they're foster-parents. But if you agree with me, and give me your permission, then I'll make the necessary arrangements for Dr Spencer, the Child Psychologist, to visit the school . . . '

Mrs Chapman's spirits lifted. This sounded promising. Something positive was happening at last. She began to feel bad about thinking the school didn't care.

'Yes, I think that would be a good idea, Mr Roper. We've tried everything. We've given him love—or tried to—and our attention, and we've tried to make his life as trouble-free as possible; but all to no use, it seems. If a doctor could help . . . '

She suddenly doubted even the magic of medicine,

132

and momentarily her spirits dropped as rapidly as they had lifted.

'Do you think a doctor can help, Mr Roper?'

The headmaster was not at all sure, but he put on a brave face.

'I certainly hope so, Mrs Chapman. But, look, if you leave it with me for a day or so, I'll have a word with Dr Spencer, fix up with her to come, and then I'll let you know.'

'Yes, that should be all right,' Mrs Chapman replied.

'Fine, Mrs Chapman, fine. I'll get on to it, then. In the meantime, try not to worry too much. Worry only communicates itself to the child, you know. Goodbye.'

Mrs Chapman's reply was cut off short as the headmaster cleared the line with his finger and immediately dialled the familiar number of the Education Office. There was no time like the present. If he didn't do something when he thought of it, it didn't get done. And it was about time he did something to sort out this Croft lad. If only there were forty hours in every day . . .

Mrs Chapman replaced her telephone and sat down at the table before making herself a pot of tea. Good, she thought, something's being done at last. Something to sort out this poor kid. And about time too. It wasn't his fault, poor little mite, but he was changing them all. Ted, herself, Keith—especially Keith. Sometimes she didn't know Keith. He wasn't her roaring, thumping Keith any more. He was more quiet, more inside himself, more like Donovan. Yes, it was about time something got done . . .

Dave and Tony had seen a change in Chapman too. He wasn't their mate any more, not after that first day in the playground. But he'd changed his character as well as his friendship.

'He's not like he used to be, up for a laugh and a muck

about,' Dave complained to his big brother who knew Alan Chapman, Keith's older brother. 'He's gone all serious, all goody-goody over that daft black kid. Soon as someone else came along he didn't want to know me and Tone. Wouldn't go out to play. Tried to get in with the older kids. Started that fight with me over nothing. He's turned right off. Worse thing of all is, now he's gone soft!'

'Well, old Alan was a bit of a mummy's boy underneath,' put in Dave's brother. 'But he'd stick by you in a fight . . . '

'Down the pool he showed it worst,' Dave went on. 'When Croft wasn't with him. Chapman shared a changing-box with this other kid, Bell, next to us . . . '

'Who, George Bell's little brother?'

'Yeah, and he's a real scruff. Odd socks he wears, and holes in his pants and long shirts. His swimming stuff's always falling out of his towel. He gets all his clothes everywhere. No one won't share with him if they can help it. Anyway, Chapman got him, and they ended up in a real mess. Chapman finished up with one sock on and one in his hand which wasn't his.'

Dave laughed explosively.

'Anyway, Bell cleared off to line up and Chapman was left in the box. Moaning like hell, he was, about the sock. "Smelly thing," he said, "'s not mine. Bell's gone off with mine!" Laugh! Tone nearly peed himself, because we could see this sock on the floor under the box. It was all in the wet. So we hooked it out with a coat-hanger and dropped it in the deep end . . . '

Dave's brother got up and switched the television on. 'Just like you,' he said. 'Rotten little swine.'

But Dave was still laughing. 'Anyway, Chapman knew we'd done it. He saw my sleeve under the box. And he came out right stroppy. "Get it out!" he said. "You put it in so you get it out." But Tone didn't feel like it, nor did

I. So I went up to him. "Want bother?" I said. That's when he went all soft. Just called us "Infants" and fished it out himself. Backed right down.'

Dave settled in his chair to watch the television.

'Not like Chapman really. Last term he'd have chucked me in . . .'

'Pity he didn't.'

'Shame. He used to be all right . . .'

12

Fewster's, the corner shop not far from Keith's street, was both a local centre of colour and a link with the world outside the criss-crossed terraces of the neighbourhood. While the small display window gathered dust on its faded crêpe paper and dummy boxes of chocolates, the shop doorway was alive with exotic magazines and a topical rack of newspaper headlines. Outside, against the low wall, a placard advertised 'Mooney's Coaches'—tempting trips out of the dull streets on to the coastal roads to the sun, a dream of paradise for those who never went. 'Southend', 'Clacton', 'Margate', and even 'Torquay' were from time to time chalked invitingly in broad coloured lettering on the blackboard. In the winter months it was 'City East Away' or 'London Theatres': always a promise of something different and exciting. But the real contact with the world at large, certainly the most dramatic, was the *Evening Standard* board which stood next to it. Here every afternoon, just about the time the children were walking home from school, a bold printed headline first proclaimed the worst (or the best) of the day's news. Often the children would walk past without seeing it. 'City Prices Slump' and 'Deadlock on Pay' had nothing to do with them. But 'Famous TV Actor Dead' or 'Murder Hunt in London Streets' seemed somehow to rivet the attention, even if it was always something of a disappointment to find later that the actor had never been heard of, or that the streets weren't racing with wailing cars: but for a while a national event had its effect in City East.

On the Monday of Mrs Chapman's phone-call to Mr Roper, Keith and Donovan walked home from school along the shaded pavement to Fewster's shop, Donovan hands in pockets and silent, Keith dribbling a tennis ball beside him. It almost seemed a shame that the *Evening Standard* headline should disturb the calm.

'LEAGUE CUP DRAW' it shouted. 'LOCAL CLASHES.'

As every boy at Transport Avenue knew, City East had made it through to the next round in an easy away game with a lower league side the previous Saturday. Keith now remembered that his father had talked of today's draw before going to work.

'We can't win the Cup,' he had said, 'but a big club here at home in the next round would suit us very nicely.'

Keith, with two pence to spend, picked up his tennis ball and hurried into the shop. Already a group of small children were hovering over the plastic tray of cheap half penny and penny items—blackjack, bubblegum and lollipops. As he joined them, Keith cast his eye over the early editions of the evening papers on the counter.

'IT'S CHELSEA V ARSENAL' read the main headline, and under it, only slightly smaller, 'CITY EAST GET PARK LANE—AT HOME'.

Keith let out a loud and sudden whoop, making the children turn indignantly—and getting a cautionary 'Steady on, son,' from Mr Fewster.

'It's Park Lane at City East,' he said, 'in the League Cup. Park Lane down here!'

He jumped up and down for joy.

'All right, all right,' said Mr Fewster, who hadn't jumped for anything for years. 'Anyone'd think they stood a chance of winning.'

'Doesn't matter,' said Keith. 'Be a good game, though!'

The great thing was, he told himself as he slipped out of the shop without buying anything, he'd be able to go and see it. After a year or so of mediocre teams from the Third Division he would at last go along to see the big names from the First, the famous familiar faces which Donovan saw every other week. A thrill of anticipation ran through him. Things were looking up.

Donovan was waiting outside the shop, with the air and the patience of a totter's horse outside a house. As soon as Keith came into view, he moved off at his slow, even pace without a word being said. But Keith soon shattered the silence.

'Hey, Don, your team's coming down, in the Cup. Park Lane's at City East in the third round. Isn't it great? We'll be able to go and see it, I expect. My dad'll take us. Just think, Park Lane down here in our ground. Great! Great!'

Keith ran and jumped along the pavement ahead of Donovan. He scored a couple of headed goals into privet hedges, and dribbled through a team of invisible Park Lane players between two lamp-posts.

'And it's Chapman with the ball, selling a dummy to Bradford, taking Wall on the blind side, playing the game of his life here at the City East ground, going through on his own, beating one man, two men, three men, and letting fly with a cannon-ball shot from the edge of the box! Pow!'

He leaned his body forward, both arms straight out for balance like a bird in flight, and cracked the imaginary ball home into the bottom left-hand corner of the net.

'And Chapman scores!' he yelled. 'It's a goal! A fantastic goal!'

He suddenly stopped his exuberant imaginings and turned to wait for the other boy. Donovan walked at his steady pace towards him, his face as impassive as ever. Keith thought wistfully of Dave and Tony. They'd have joined in and played a whole imaginary match, three commentators shouting their own versions of the game all the way home.

'Anyway, my dad'll be pleased,' Keith said suddenly. 'About the draw. Bet yours will be too: easy game for Park Lane.'

There was no reaction from Donovan, so Keith said no more about the game until his dad came home from work. Mr Chapman had known about the draw since mid-day, and he had further news of the big match.

'One of the lads phoned the ground,' he said. 'It's going to be an all-ticket game—vouchers in next week's home programme. We'll have to go along and get some programmes and then queue up on Sunday morning to buy the tickets. No programme voucher, no ticket. Lot of rigmarole, isn't it?'

He sat in the armchair and turned to the back page of his evening paper.

'Anyway, Ted Dixon says City East have got a grand chance of a surprise win.' He laughed scornfully. 'Ever the optimist, the City East Manager!'

There was silence for a few moments.

'Still, it'll be a good game,' said Keith.

'Oh, it'll be well worth my money,' said Mr Chapman. 'And yours.'

He winked at Keith. For a minute or two he went on reading his paper. Then he suddenly lowered it and turned in his chair to look up at the other boy in the room. Donovan had been standing by the corner of the table looking solemnly across at him since he had first sat down.

'Do you want to come, Donovan?' he asked kindly. 'To the match? City East against Park Lane?'

The three Chapmans looked intently at Donovan, as they always did when a direct question was put to him. Mr Chapman felt hopeful. Donovan was looking straight at him. Their eyes made contact, the man's face eager and open, the boy's closed. But Mr Chapman remembered that moment upstairs in Donovan's room when he had talked about the Park Lane photograph, before the disappointment. Once again he had that optimistic feeling that he was about to see some movement from Donovan. Just a slight almost imperceptible nod. It seemed no more than a twitch away. Again he raised his eyebrows enquiringly and smiled encouragement. They all held the silence for a few tense seconds. Then, as before, the moment passed. It might very nearly have been a nod. Nobody could know.

'Well, I'll get you a ticket anyway,' Ted Chapman said. 'We'll all go.'

Dr Spencer's coming was always a mixed blessing to Mr Roper. It often led to greater understanding and help for a child; but for a whole morning it also entailed the loss of his room. The headmaster's room was the only quiet place where the psychologist could work without interruption, but it meant that Mr Roper had to gather his morning's needs and share the small converted stock-cupboard which his secretary used. Everyone in the school knew, on these occasions, that he was homeless and therefore much more likely to make unannounced visits to the classrooms. Twelve classes of children were held on a tight rein for the morning. Mr Harper, the caretaker, often had his boiler-room inspected at about the time he brewed his tea; and the school cook had her menus discussed at coffee time.

Dr Spencer arrived in her sports car and, leaving a vapour trail of perfume, was led by a helpful child to Mr Roper. Unlike the teachers, though, she never let anyone carry her bag. An unhappy experience in a school for disturbed girls had left its mark early in her career. Her smiling greeting for Mr Roper began when they were half the length of the hall apart.

'Mr Roper, good morning, so nice to see you,' she purred, eventually shaking hands with a clicking of wooden bracelets. 'And such a lovely day.' Mr Roper murmured a greeting and followed her into his room. Seeing his desk clear she sat behind it. Mr Roper drew up a chair before her. He always felt less important when Dr Spencer came.

She got straight to the point.

'Now, Donovan Croft,' she said, without referring to her notes. 'You told me all about him on the phone. Any change in his behaviour? Any speech yet, Mr Roper?'

She stroked him with his name, smoothing the ruffled fur.

'No, I'm afraid not. No change whatsoever. I must say I find it hard to imagine what anyone can do . . . '

Dr Spencer frowned. 'Well, we'll see, Mr Roper, we'll see. Now, did you manage to make the appointments I asked you to make? With the foster-mother, and the natural father?' She smiled across at him sweetly.

'Yes. I've given you an hour and a half with Donovan, as you asked, then Mrs Chapman is coming later. When I saw her last time I asked her to contact the boy's real father and ask him to come too . . . '

'Good,' interjected the psychologist, still giving Mr Roper all her attention.

' . . . but I haven't heard whether or not he's able to come: we'll have to wait and see, I'm afraid . . . '

'Yes, of course, we'll wait and see.'

Dr Spencer started to unzip a rather fat briefcase.

'But it would be most useful to talk to the father. All

right? Then we'll begin, and take tea at, say, ten to eleven? Will that be all right?'

'Yes, I'll organize it,' Mr Roper agreed, getting up and taking a last look round the room to see if he had forgotten anything. 'Sugar and milk?'

'How kind; yes, please, Mr Roper . . . and if at all possible, a little digestive biscuit. That would be most kind.'

Mr Roper could only nod.

'Well now, I'll see Donovan Croft, alone, and if possible, Mr Roper, without interruption. You understand, don't you?'

From her briefcase she took some coloured bricks with patterns on them and began setting them on the desk in front of her.

'Thank you very much.'

'I'll get him now,' the headmaster said, and made a swift exit from the room. 'Ruddy cheek,' he murmured as he crept round the back of the lesson in the hall to get Donovan from his classroom. 'Treats me like the office boy.'

Donovan went mutely with him back to the office: if he wondered why he was going there he certainly didn't show it to the headmaster. At his own door, Mr Roper knocked. Dr Spencer opened it and ushered Donovan in like a very welcome guest.

'Come in, Donovan,' she said, 'and make yourself at home. I'm Dr Spencer, and I want to talk to you, and then I want you to do some puzzles for me. All right?' She didn't give Donovan time not to answer. 'Fine, well now you come and sit over here.'

She gave him the chair opposite her own and as Mr Roper discreetly shut the door on them, she began her tests. She knew better than to expect Donovan suddenly to start talking to her, but she did ask him several questions to which he might have nodded or shaken his head in answer. He did neither, however; he simply sat with his hands in his lap and his eyes on the coloured bricks on the desk.

'Now, have I got it right? Your name is Donovan, isn't it?'

No response from Donovan.

'And you're living at the moment with Mr and Mrs Chapman?'

No response.

'Your father works very hard, doesn't he?'

No response.

'And I see that your mum has gone to Jamaica to nurse your grandad. Is that right?'

Again, Donovan failed to respond—on the outside at least. Inside, though, at the mention of his mother, his stomach felt acutely again the real pain of wanting, a dropping, churning sensation as if he were falling from a great height.

'Well, I'd like you to do some drawings and puzzles for me, Donovan.'

Dr Spencer gave him a plain sheet of paper and a soft-lead black pencil. At the top of the paper Donovan's name had been typed, together with the date and the name of the school.

When he had the paper before him he was asked to draw a man on it, any man he liked but as well as he could. Without glancing up, he drew the picture: a tall man in a jumper and slacks, facing the front with his arms by his side. It didn't look like anyone Donovan knew. As soon as he had finished the picture the paper was taken swiftly away from him with a clicking of bracelets and another, larger, sheet of paper replaced it. On this Donovan was asked to draw his family. Again, his figures faced the front, Mum on the left, Donovan in the middle, Dad on the right. Dad and Mum looked very tall, Donovan a smallish figure between them.

Dr Spencer said that they were good. But the praise meant nothing to Donovan. He simply sat, still and hunched, waiting for the next instruction.

Next, the coloured bricks had to be arranged in various patterns, according to some photographs in a little coloured booklet. It was easy at first, but the patterns got harder and harder, and Donovan wasn't at all sure about the last few. Finally, Dr Spencer said a long series of words to Donovan, and Donovan had to point to the one picture on a page of four which was described by the word. Again, this was easy at first, but it became harder as the list went on.

At last Dr Spencer had finished. With long red-tipped fingers she scooped the papers together and stood up. She held out her right hand to be shaken, smiling across at him, wrinkling her eyes behind her thick black spectacle frames.

'Goodbye, Donovan,' she said. She took his hand and shook it. 'Did you enjoy that?'

But the handshake was as far as Donovan's injured will was prepared to go. His eyes settled again on the bricks, distant, his mind a thousand miles away.

'You can go back to your class now. You've been a very good boy.'

Donovan walked out of the room and closed the door behind him. He turned to go down the narrow wooden steps to the hall, his eyes on the floor. There was a chair in the way. Donovan side-stepped and looked up. Then he stopped dead in his tracks. Sitting on the chair, getting up to greet him with a big smile on his face, was a very familiar figure. It was his father.

There could be no mistaking it was Donovan's father: he had the same bone structure, strong yet somehow delicately shaped cheek-bones, prominent eyebrows and a squarish well-formed nose. A point of difference was the short neat black moustache which grew thinly on his upper lip. In a flared grey three-piece suit he looked very smart, with the purple-dot tie and matching handkerchief which Donovan's mother had bought him at Christmas.

The tall man threw his arms round Donovan and hugged him to his waistcoated chest.

'Hallo, boy,' he said, his voice deep but somehow uncertain, like a blues singer with a tender lyric. 'How you been going then? I left you to it, like I thought best, but I missed you, son.'

Donovan stood still against his father, his arms by his sides, his weight pulled forwards on to his toes by the big man's tender rocking.

'I know you've been a good boy, Donovan. Mrs Chapman told me in a letter all about you. But why don't you talk to no one, son? You've got no reason not to talk . . . '

He released the boy and, pressing his big palms against Donovan's cheeks, he tilted his face up to look into his own.

'Well, come on now, Donovan, say hallo to your daddy . . . '

Donovan looked up into his father's face, seeing his own reflection in the man's liquid brown eyes. It seemed an age, and yet at the same time only yesterday, since he had seen that very familiar face.

'Come on then, son, say hallo to your daddy . . . '

Donovan closed his own eyes and pulled his head down, overcoming the pressure of his father's hands. He stood looking through half-closed misty eyes at the small pattern on his father's waistcoat.

Mr Croft renewed the pressure of his hands on Donovan's cheeks, tilting his head up again.

146

'Now, Donovan, you can say hallo to your daddy—can't you?'

There was a hint of impatience now in his father's voice. Donovan closed his eyes again. Mr Croft stood and waited. The boy was acting very silly, he thought.

Fortunately, Dr Spencer broke the impasse. She had opened the door some moments before and watched the unhappy scene. Now it was time to bring it to an end.

'Hallo, Mr Croft, I'm Dr Spencer. It was very kind of you to come.' She rattled a hand out to Mr Croft. 'Do please come in. You must say goodbye to Donovan for a little while. We can arrange for you to see him again when we've had our chat.'

Donovan's father looked over the boy's head at the psychologist, his eyes pained and bewildered; he had thought his own presence was all the boy had needed. It was a deep and painful shock to find a ravine of distrust between his son and himself. He released his pressure on Donovan's face.

'Yes, doctor, good morning.' He looked down again at his son. 'I'll see you in a while, boy,' he said. 'I'll see you here. OK?'

Donovan remained mute and unmoved. His father stepped round him slowly and went over to the headmaster's door. Dr Spencer took him gently by the arm and led him through the doorway.

'Come along, Mr Croft. Let's have our chat.'

Mr Croft looked over his shoulder at his son. The boy was walking slowly down the steps, away from him. In a distant part of the building a hand-bell rang, denoting playtime, and the first feet were heard on the turret stairs.

'Come back after play, Donovan,' Dr Spencer called, 'and see your father again before he goes back to work . . .'

The boy walked across the empty hall, and Mr Croft turned back into Mr Roper's room. He pulled his purple-spotted handkerchief from his breast pocket and dabbed at his eyes.

'Doctor, doctor, what can we do?' he asked.

No one disliked sad meetings more than Dr Spencer; but she was pleased the meeting between Donovan and his father had taken place when she realized how deeply it had affected Mr Croft. Later, she was certain it led him to tell her more about the family split-up than he might otherwise have done.

She spent the first five minutes, while his thoughts were still outside the door, putting him at his ease. Then at the end of a series of routine enquiries about the family, she put the question which she was sure held the key to the mystery of Donovan's muteness.

'Mr Croft, why did your wife go away to Jamaica so suddenly? I think it would help me to know.'

She knew by the man's eyes that his first impulse was to tell her less than the truth; his eyes also told her when he finally began speaking that he was being painfully honest with her.

What Mr Croft had to say did not altogether surprise her. She had suspected that something more than a family visit to Jamaica by his mother had triggered off Donovan's unhappiness.

In the course of a long and unhappy explanation, Mr Croft told her of the letter they had suddenly received from Jamaica during July. It contained news of the serious illness, and the impending death, of Mrs Croft's father. Mr Croft had comforted his wife, and sympathized with her, but he had been shocked to find her making plans to fly home to the West Indies, for it involved spending all their savings: the money they hoped to put towards a deposit on a house of their own some day. It was stupid, Mr Croft thought, because her father would be bound to be dead before she could get there. But Mrs Croft had insisted on going, and she had seen her husband's attempts to stop her as both selfish and mean. Then the arguments had begun—kept from Donovan, but continuing throughout the couple of weeks it took to draw the money from the post office and get the passport renewed. None of Mr Croft's attempts to dissuade her—arguments that they had cut themselves off from Jamaica, that their life and future lay in England—could make her change her mind. She said that at this time of crisis she had to go home. And at the end of a long, bitter quarrel one hot night, Mrs Croft had suddenly packed her bags and gone.

It was easy for Dr Spencer, an outsider, to see how Donovan's mother had been unable to cut herself off from the past as completely as her husband had done, and this was the difference between them. This was the chasm between the two into which Donovan had fallen, by which he had been injured.

So, with the story told in all its detail, Mr Croft stopped speaking. He suddenly sat back in his chair as if snapping himself back to the present and dismissing the regrets of the past. There was little more he could tell the doctor. She knew it all now. Dr Spencer also sat back, leaning into her chair and gazing at the ceiling as she considered what to say. She took her glasses off and rubbed her eyes.

'Well first, Mr Croft, I'm going to tell you what I think is wrong with Donovan—and believe me, there's some cause for concern. Then I'm going to tell you what I think you can do about it. OK?'

He nodded.

She leaned forward in her chair now and began speaking slowly and softly to the man opposite her. She talked to him for nearly ten minutes without pausing. She ignored a knock on the door, Mr Roper's head round it even, forfeiting her cup of tea and digestive biscuit. But what she said was important and had to be understood.

She told Mr Croft that Donovan was a normal, intelligent boy, but he had had a terrible shock. From relative happiness his family life had slid to abject misery. His mother had seemed to desert him—which after so many years of loving must have been a monstrous blow to take—and shortly after her departure his father had had to send him away, appearing to reject him too. It was little wonder, the doctor said, that he wanted to have no more to do with people when they treated him like that. This was the reason for his loss of speech. And only by someone putting this situation right could Donovan have any chance of regaining it.

'Mr Croft, I take it that you can't have Donovan home again? I mean, there's no question of you giving up your job for a spell?'

Donovan's father shook his head. His gesture and facial expression gave the strong impression of a man pulling out his pocket linings to show how broke he was.

'Well then, you'll have to do it at weekends, by visiting him, by taking him out, by trying to recapture the happiness he had with you, by letting him do the things he did with you, by his just being near you as much as the circumstances allow . . .'

The tall man felt choked with the frustration of knowing he could do all this and more if it weren't for the tight bonds of his job. And the fact that he had been wrong to leave Donovan to make his way with the Chapmans on his own was hard to swallow. It was just that he had thought that best, not to dangle home in front of him, visiting then going away.

'Can you think of any situation you can create,

anything you can do with him which will help him to feel that things haven't really changed—that you still love him and want to be with him?'

Mr Croft sat thinking, a frown of concentration wrinkling his brow. This was very difficult. Dr Spencer prompted him.

'Did you go fishing together? Or out cycling? Or did you share any hobbies—like model railways, or pigeons, or football . . . ?'

As if a puppeteer had pulled his string, Mr Croft sat up, his eyes wide with an idea.

'Football!' he said. 'We go to football, him and me, every home game we go to Park Lane . . . '

But then he slumped back again as the string was cut above him.

' . . . but I don't get the time to get over here and take him back to the ground Saturdays.' He sighed. 'I work till one on Saturday, my regular job, and if I don't work I don't get kept on . . . '

Dr Spencer pursued her point. It was sometimes difficult to get people to understand what things they should put first—although she could see that the man obviously couldn't afford to lose his job.

'Well, perhaps you can work something out. Perhaps Mr Chapman could bring him up to meet you once or twice. Do think about it, Mr Croft, because that's the only hope there is: to help him to return to a state of being wanted, of being loved. He's got to feel really loved by someone. If you can do that then he might want to come back into our world again. A real feeling of security, doing something he likes with you, might just provide the stimulus we need . . . '

Mr Croft nodded. 'Yes, ma'am. I see. I think I can do what you want . . . '

'It's not what I want, Mr Croft,' said Dr Spencer,

standing up. 'It's what your son needs. That's the whole point, isn't it?'

'Yes, I know. Yes, doctor,' replied the chastened father. 'I'll do what he needs.'

Dr Spencer could see that he meant it; he meant it desperately. She came round the desk and opened the door.

'And there is one thing you can do—for the pair of you . . .'

'Yes?' He tidied his breast-pocket handkerchief and tightened the knot of his tie.

'You can write to your wife, and ask her to come home—as soon as she can. As soon as things are settled in Jamaica.'

The sad man stood in the doorway, thinking, his eyes on his shining black shoes. Then he looked up at her.

'Thank you, doctor, I've done that.'

'Good luck, Mr Croft,' she said. She smiled at him. 'And don't give up too easily. It may take some time.'

Once outside the door, Mr Croft drew a deep unsteady breath. This morning had been almost as unnerving as the original departure of his wife. Then his world had been stood on its head. Now it was going into a flat spin.

He looked round the small platform for Donovan, but there was no sign of the boy. He sat on a chair with his elbows on his knees and his head in his hands and waited for him to reappear. He felt sick inside and the nerves behind his eyes began to ache with the frustration of being unable to do what he most wanted, to take the boy back home and be his real father again. Any other way could only be second best.

But as he sat there and waited, he began to realize that even second best was hard to achieve, Donovan wasn't coming back to say goodbye. Whether he could not, or would not, Mr Croft didn't know. All he knew, as his headache grew worse and the boy did not appear, was that the time at his disposal, the time reluctantly granted off from work, was rapidly running out, and if he was to get over to the other side of the city in time he would have to leave now and drive as fast as the traffic conditions would allow.

Frustrated, depressed, and despondent, knowing his son was near by but not accessible to him, he jingled his car keys in a nervous gesture and headed for the school doors. So that was that.

As the bright light of the outside hit his eyes with a sudden stab of pain, he dropped his head and hurried to the car. He passed Mrs Chapman walking in, but neither knew the other and they didn't speak. She might have guessed, though. There couldn't be many men at the school that morning with a reason for leaving in tears.

13

The meeting with his father seemed to have put Donovan back, if that were possible. He returned to his classroom, both surprised at having seen the man from his old world here in the present one, and strangely upset, even at his father's appearance. Donovan always pictured him wearing his familiar working clothes, or his weekend jacket and cords; but this smart, sharp suit had no connection with the boy. He had seen it before, but it had never seemed like his dad in it. Mr Croft had worn it once or twice to go out to dances, and once to a nightclub—all occasions when a neighbour had come in and watched television with Donovan while his parents had gone out into a private world of their own. But he had never felt any resentment until now.

He sat at his desk and stared at the exercise-book in front of him, his stomach turning over, his memory stirred up again like the dirt at the bottom of a puddle. Pencil in hand, he made no more than a token effort to do any work. He felt muddled and frustrated. He wanted to see his dad, and he didn't; he had felt good being held close to him again, and he had been upset. Why? Was it because his father wanted his love, but he didn't want to have to look after him? Did his dad care, or was he putting on a show for these people? A few weeks ago such questions could never in the world have occurred to him. Now the answers were vital to his happiness.

There was a loud and sudden snap as the point of Donovan's pencil broke under the pressure of his push against the desk. Wordlessly, without looking up from the desk he was bending over to mark a book, Mr Henry slipped a fresh pencil out of his top pocket and laid it in Donovan's groove. It was an automatic gesture, like putting a dummy back into a baby's mouth. Hardly anyone spoke to Donovan any more: communication is a two-way business.

As they walked home after school that day, Keith noticed a subtle change in Donovan: he was walking more slowly, he made no effort to keep abreast or to cross the roads with Keith, his chin was sunk lower on his chest, his shoulders drooped just half-an-inch more. Keith's keen sense of mood, undeveloped before Donovan came, was tuned now to register a deeper depression, a further coiling into the shell.

As usual he left Donovan to himself for a while when they first got indoors. Keith knew Donovan liked to feed Fluff, a chore which he had willingly given up, so when the boy went out of the back door, Keith grabbed a handful of biscuits and sprawled flat on his stomach in front of the television to watch a Laurel and Hardy film. It was funny, and he rolled over on the carpet, his stomach heaving in laughter; his mother ticked him off for spraying the floor with biscuit crumbs as he snorted explosively with amusement. But his laughter was infectious, and Mrs Chapman caught the germ. She smiled while Keith collapsed, and she forgot to be cross about the mess. He made so much noise that it wasn't until she went to the kitchen for a dustpan and brush that she heard the great commotion that was coming from the garden.

Donovan first lost the guinea-pig when he was putting it back into its hutch. He had cleaned out the main living area and put down fresh straw; he had topped up the water hopper and put fresh pellets into the food dish; he had taken Fluff out for a cuddle and stroke. Somehow, though, he had done it all in a sad sort of dream state, his mind a long way off, which wasn't typical of his daily dealings with Fluff. Perhaps he held the guinea-pig a little too tightly; perhaps his stroking was not as gentle as usual; for when he came to put the creature back into the hutch he misjudged the distance and Fluff, by now feeling insecure and uncertain in the boy's hands, tried to jump the small gap, missed, and fell to the ground.

Donovan crouched down to pick up the frightened animal. It was standing trembling violently, making no attempt to evade him, like a hedgehog caught in headlights. Within a second or two Donovan would have retrieved it; but just at that moment Fluff heard the next-to-silent sound of a cat moving: a cat tensing its muscles from a languid relaxed state on the warm soil, to an alert, pouncing position; a cat not a metre from where the guinea-pig shook. Donovan's ears picked up the low throaty growl of the aroused and interested cat, and he looked round to see the sharp, fox-like head of Mrs Parsons' black cat, Tommy, easing its weight forward on three legs. It froze just like that, its fourth, leading, paw coyly curled in anticipation of the swift swipe which was to come—any second from now.

Thinking quickly, Donovan lunged for the cat, catching it on the nose with the back of his hand, and the guinea-pig scampered away from the danger area as fast as its small legs could carry it. It ran under Donovan's falling body and across the small cement path towards the flower-bed on the south side of the narrow garden. It scuttled away beneath the leaves of a rhubarb plant and found a refuge somewhere at the bottom of the fence by Mrs Parsons' garden.

The cat leapt two lengths backwards and chased round Donovan's body with the speed and grace of a jaguar. A cat running off in fright is comical; the same creature on the hunt is menacing and sleekly beautiful. This was Tommy, proud and deadly. Sensing the best vantage point he leapt to the top of the two-metre fence in one bound and silhouetted himself in a searching position along the woodwork, his four feet now in a straight and perfectly balanced line, like an Egyptian wall painting.

Nothing moved for a few moments; but the hunter often relies on a rash dash for safety by the hunted. So Tommy waited on the fence, while Donovan crouched upon the path. Then, at ground level, Fluff made a strategic mistake and broke cover. He made his run, but instead of running for home, back across the narrow space towards Donovan and the hutch, he scuttled through a hole in the fence and exposed a clear target to the predator above as he zigzagged across Mr Parsons' mint patch towards a thick clump of grass which grew round the base of the clothes-line pole.

Donovan stood up just in time to see Tommy taking a vertical dive down the other side of the fence, purposeful and sinister. Without stopping to consider what he was doing, Donovan ran across the narrow garden and shinned over the fence in a slick but noisy commando leap— the most positive movement his body had made in a month.

By crashing loudly on the fence with his toe-caps, Donovan made Tommy pause for two or three seconds in bewilderment, darting his head round to stare at the boy with sharp, intelligent eyes. It was just long enough to allow Donovan to see the relative positions of cat and guinea-pig: a short freezing of the action in which Donovan began his leap down into the Parsons' garden.

The arrival of this earth-shaking shape from the sky caused Tommy to draw back, as cautious and discreet as all his species, while Donovan lunged at the petrified guinea-pig like a cricketer going for a low catch. His grab was good and his other hand came to support the first in a swift cupping motion which both captured and protected, holding the guinea-pig down against the thick-bladed grass.

Tommy, knowing defeat but impervious to failure as only the superior can be, loped off to lick his ruffled fur among the wall-flowers—while the centre of the garden was left to Donovan, to Fluff—and, suddenly, to Mrs Parsons.

'You little swine,' she said, advancing towards Donovan with her hand raised, 'what the hell are you doing over here?'

She was so angry that she couldn't get the breath to shout as loudly as she wanted, as in a nightmare when her call for help came out silently. She wanted to knock the little swine's block off. But she had more sense. Oh, no, they knew how to make trouble, this sort. So she stood over him, but with her hand still raised.

'I told you before, I don't want you over here,' her voice shrilled at him, gaining strength as the first indignant shock of seeing him there wore off. 'What're you doing over here, eh? Eh? Don't give a damn for nobody's property. Take, take, take, it's the only bloody word you know.'

Donovan stood up slowly, careful not to drop Fluff again under this new pressure. Mrs Parsons' hand stayed level with his head as she drew a deep angry breath for her next burst of invective. He turned his head away from her, his eyes closed, and a hand held up protectively in front of him. The sun hid its eyes behind a chimney-stack and threw a hard, chill shadow across the scrub of garden.

'You're not fit to wipe my boots!' Mrs Parsons shouted.

Donovan stood stock still, waiting for the hand to come slapping into the side of his head. But when her hand moved, it was not in a slap but in a wild gesture of dismissal.

'Go on, get out!' she shrieked. 'I've told you before. Get back where you belong . . .'

Donovan began to move back towards the fence over which he had climbed, Fluff still clutched firmly against his stomach with one hand.

'Not over the fence!' Mrs Parsons hit a new shrill ceiling of sound with her indignation. 'Go round!'

Donovan changed direction and began walking down the garden to the small gate at the bottom, his head bent low, his pace slow with defeat and utter hopelessness. Mrs Parsons stood watching him go. The insolent little swine, mooching off like that. As if she was nothing, a doormat, riff-raff. Her anger welled up again.

'Go on!' she screamed, almost out of control, but retaining sufficient to choose her words with care. 'You black waste of space!'

'Mrs Parsons!'

Keith's mother had reached her neighbour's garden gate along the back alley. She and Keith had been attracted out by the sound of Mrs Parsons' shrill voice, and hearing the words being used, she had guessed that Donovan was involved. She had taken the quickest route she could to the scene of the trouble, but Keith had found a quicker way and was already up on the fence.

As Donovan came towards the gate his hurt showed clearly. He was still clutching the guinea-pig, but his eyes were half-closed, and running down his cheeks were two courses of large bitter tears. His mouth was slightly open and as he heaved his shoulders uncontrollably in silent sobs, the dribble ran over his chin.

'Keith!' Mrs Chapman shouted, flaring up herself. 'Take the boy in while I sort this stupid woman out!'

Mrs Parsons had never seen her neighbour roused like this before. As the angry Mrs Chapman advanced up her garden towards her, she backed away involuntarily at first; then when she bumped into the line post she defiantly stood her ground. An Englishwoman's home is her castle.

'You're trespassing!' she shouted in her shrill voice. 'Go on, you're trespassing!'

Mrs Chapman came up to within a metre of her. She hadn't been this angry with an outsider since she'd been a girl at school.

'You'll be lucky if that's the only crime I'm guilty of,' she gasped, 'before I'm finished with you.' She waved a finger in Mrs Parsons' bewildered face. 'That poor kid needs help, not abuse from you . . . I hope you're proud of yourself, a grown woman like you shouting at a kid like that . . . Didn't you hear my husband tell you before, he's ill . . . ?'

'You're trespassing!' put in Mrs Parsons. 'I hope you know you're trespassing!'

'That boy needs love and kindness, not your sort of ignorant prejudice . . . '

'Trespassing, you are . . . '

Mrs Chapman suddenly stopped. She looked at her neighbour's red face, her bulging eyes, her scornful mouth about to spit out once more that the other was trespassing. Mrs Chapman dropped her voice, and in a harsh hiss, using a word which had been a stranger to her since her schooldays, she spoke her final words to Mrs Parsons:

'You make me ashamed to be white . . . bloody ashamed!'

Then she turned on her heel and strode out of the alien garden.

Keith put an arm round Donovan and walked him back up their own garden to the hutch. Donovan's body heaved with a sob every step or so, and he nearly dropped the guinea-pig again at the hutch: together the boys put the creature in, and then with Keith's arm to steer and comfort him, Donovan walked indoors.

Keith took Donovan into the living-room and sat him down in the fireside armchair. His cheeks were as wet with tears as if he had held his face under a tap. His nose was running and the back of his hands shone with moisture where he had wiped the dribble away. His eyes, closed and puffy, dripped with misery and his hunched shoulders shook.

Keith sat on the side of the chair and put his arm round his foster-brother's shoulder again. He didn't know what to say; he wasn't very experienced in the world and dealing with this abject misery was something new again for him; but he began to speak softly, and he went on talking till the sobbing ceased.

'She's a silly old cow, Don. You don't want to take no notice of her. You're worth ten of her. Don't worry. She's a right old misery. She's the same with me. She never gives me my tennis balls back unless Dad has a go at her, and she always bangs on my wall if I jump on the bed . . . '

He took a screwed-up tissue out of the pocket of his jeans and put it in Donovan's ineffectually wiping hands.

'She's always had a thing about black people. She's got a real thing about them. Does her nut. She's stupid. Honest, Don, she's not worth bothering about . . . '

He shifted his position and leaned down nearer the other boy, holding him tighter round the shoulders.

'She can't hurt you. Nor can old Henry, nor can anyone. No one can. Not while you're my . . . sort of . . . my brother. You're my brother while you're here. And we're together, you and me. And we stick together . . . '

He looked into the boy's face. Donovan was quieter now.

'Get it? It's you and me. If anyone tries to get one of us, it's you and me. See?' He paused. 'OK, Don? You and me. OK?'

Keith looked down at the other's face. Donovan had lowered his hands. His eyes were open, looking up at Keith. Suddenly, they filled over again with moisture, almost a voluntary squeezing gesture of answer. Donovan had heard words like that before: long before, in the happy days: words his mam had used. They gave him a strange tingling feeling over the surface of his face and hands when he heard them again. Deliberately, fractionally, he nodded. There was no mistake. He slowly nodded at Keith.

Keith said nothing for a moment. He didn't dare. He was full up himself. Donovan had nodded to him. He could hardly believe it. That nod was as good as a speech from Don. Poor old Don. Poor kid. He just wanted a mate. A real mate, that was all. Well, now they'd show everyone. Together they would. Now that Don was prepared to trust him.

Keith suddenly felt happy. He felt like Keith again. Keith Chapman. Himself. And in the most normal, casual, equal voice, which nonetheless shouted success at Mrs Chapman in the doorway, he slipped off the arm of the chair and told them he was going to make them all a nice cup of tea.

14

A strong invisible bond grew between the boys in the days following the Fluff episode. It was more like the thin tight wire of the secret agent than the more obvious rope of the mountaineer: but its strength was clearly felt by both boys. A strain on one end always pulled at the other. Keith was aware that it had been there for some time, but he had been frightened to put any weight on it before.

The bond became apparent in small ways. Donovan now kept up with Keith when they walked to school. When Keith ran past the 'dirty house', holding his breath for a count of twenty as usual, Donovan ran with him, not knowing why, but doing it because Keith did. In assembly there was one hymn-book between two, picked up from a pile by the classroom door as the children filed out into the hall. That next Friday morning, Donovan picked one up for the first time, and although he left Keith to find the place and he didn't sing himself, he had made his gesture of sharing.

Otherwise, although there was little change in anything they did, there was a general air of reduced tension in the Chapman household.

The event to which the Chapmans looked forward with the keenest interest, apart from the coming League Cup Tie, was the Sunday visit of Mr Croft. It had been fixed up by telephone after Dr Spencer's visit to the school, the beginning of the campaign to get father and son together again, and everyone was eager to see whether a further breakthrough, perhaps even the most important, Donovan speaking, might be made some time during the day. If he was going to speak to anyone, they all felt, it was bound to be his own father.

As it happened, everyone was disappointed. It was a wet depressing day from the start, the sort of day on which only the extreme optimist would back a horse or go fishing. A flat grey ceiling of cloud was rollered onto the sky without a break, and the steady windless drizzle sprayed a dark shine over the whole of City East.

Many of the men had spent an hour or so eight deep across the pavement at the City East football ground. With their collars turned up and wearing all sorts of improvised newsprint hats, they had endured the rain in order to get their cup tie tickets for the following Saturday. Keith and Mr Chapman had jostled in the queue for just over an hour, but they returned home satisfied with their allocation of two ground tickets each, enough for themselves and Donovan and a friend of Mr Chapman's who might be going.

They got in to find that Donovan had spent the morning lying on his bed. Mrs Chapman, hot and tired, was still cooking the roast. She didn't exactly say she could have done with a bit of help, but her disinterest in the football tickets and her monosyllabic replies told them all they needed to know. Without saying much, Mr Chapman found a job in the shed and Keith sorted his soldiers. Now they were all doing something different, each on his own, but each one of them thinking of the same thing: the coming of Mr Croft.

Unfortunately, Mr Croft arrived late. His car hadn't started in the damp without a great deal of persuasion and he had then lost his way in a Sunday-morning diversion: by the time he arrived, the dinners had all sat drying in the hot oven for twenty minutes.

When she opened the front door, Mrs Chapman gave their visitor a warm, if slightly forced, welcome—a cheerfulness which she suddenly switched on like a device to dispel the depressed atmosphere of the house. She noticed that Mr Croft had parked his car as much outside the Parsons' house as their own, and she nearly asked him to move it back. A week before she would have—they were all very conscious of their own car space in these streets without garages. Instead, she ushered him straight into the front room where the others stood waiting politely, and within five minutes they were all sitting down to eat.

Donovan and his father viewed one another through new, uncertain, eyes. They were unsure of each other now and of themselves, and they used the furniture and the Chapmans to keep them apart for a while. Mrs Chapman was glad that they all had something to do, if only the eating of a fast-cooling meal.

During the meal, Mr Croft watched his son like a hawk. He almost devoured him, watching for a sign, listening for a sound, creating an atmosphere at the table about as relaxed as that at a formal banquet at Buckingham Palace. Keith's father found conversation at the meal hard-going. He had bought some cans of beer to offer to the visitor, but Mr Croft said he didn't drink beer, only Coca-Cola, so there was no drink to help the talk to flow; and with Donovan present they certainly couldn't talk about the subject which had brought them all together.

It wasn't until Keith sneezed, and they got round to talking about football, that the conversation picked up for a bit. Mrs Chapman quickly blamed the cold which Keith had caught (she was sure) on the long queue in the rain for football tickets, and at the mention of these, Mr Croft looked away from Donovan and listened to the talk.

'You going then, boy?' he asked Donovan when he

had heard about the ticket purchases. 'You going to see the old team play down here?'

He kept a straight face, a steady voice, but inside an idea was growing; might this be the opportunity Dr Spencer had told him he had to take? With mounting excitement he knew that this could be his chance to do the old things with the boy—together on the terraces, shouting for the old team. Why not, for Pete's sake? If the game was here at City East he could make a straight run through after work and pick Donovan up on his way. That would be easy to do. And who could tell, he asked himself, it might just lead to his son talking again.

His question still hung in the air. He repeated it. 'You going then?'

Donovan did not look up from his meal, but Mr Chapman answered for him. 'Yes, we're all going, the three of us . . .'

Mr Croft sat back and smiled. He was pleased the boy was going. He could easily get a ticket and go with them, he thought. 'You're going to see a great side,' he said. 'That Park Lane team sure is something. Me and Donovan been going down there for two years—never miss the home games, do we? And without doubt they are the best team in England. No team to touch them any way.' He chuckled deeply. 'Poor old City East is in for a thrashing!'

Mr Chapman left Keith to leap loyally to their defence.

'They *could* be good,' he said, 'if they had all the money Park Lane's got, all the rich men to support them. But they'll still knock old Park Lane out. You see. Park Lane softies!'

'I don't think I'll live to see it happen,' Mr Croft laughed. 'What do you say, Donovan? It ain't possible . . . not for a million years.' He looked round the table, smiling, his gaze settling on the boy who sat with his knife and fork together and his hands in his lap. The man frowned. There was no disguising the fact. Donovan had made no move towards him at all. Dr Spencer was right. It was not going to be easy. He addressed Donovan directly again.

'What you say, eh? Shall I come with you down to City East next week? Shall I try and get a ticket?'

Donovan did not seem to hear him; but Keith did.

'We've got a spare ticket, haven't we, Dad? We only got one for Mr Waters in case he wants to go. Come with us . . .'

'Yes, come with us,' Mr Chapman agreed readily. 'We only got our full allocation on the off-chance. Good idea.'

His wife was even more enthusiastic. She gave meaningful looks to both men.

'That's a very good idea,' she said. 'It'll be just like old times for you two then, won't it, Mr Croft?'

Mr Croft nodded. It must be a good idea. They could all see it. If the boy failed to talk to his father today, next Saturday would be an ideal opportunity for them to get together again—and in a large crowd, watching Park Lane United as they had so often in the past, everyone around them shouting their support, just like old times—there was a good chance that Donovan might feel happy enough to want to speak again. It was a good opportunity, much too good to miss.

There, at that point, on that drab Sunday, the interest and the conversation ceased. Nothing more was to be achieved. The men and the boys helped to wash up, and Mr Chapman made a cup of tea while several blind alleys of talk were travelled by Mrs Chapman and Mr Croft. The two boys sat on the floor, carefully balancing their unaccustomed cups in the front room, while the clock ticked and the rain fell.

The Chapmans wondered whether Mr Croft might have taken Donovan out had the day been brighter, father and son together. But anyway, he didn't. Secretly he was too scared of another failure just yet. So they all sat round protecting the pair with their presence until Mr Chapman suddenly climbed out of the deep settee and turned the television on.

Immediately, the tension disappeared with the need to speak; the manufactured worries of *The Golden Shot* replaced their own home-grown problem for half-an-hour. They all sat engrossed in the programme, let off from talking. Even Donovan watched with interest, and, when one of the competitors won a hundred pounds, he smiled. But it was only a faint smile, and it was only seen by Keith.

When Mr Croft left an hour later he still hadn't seen any sign of life in Donovan's face.

'Like a stranger,' he kept saying to himself as he drove home through the Sunday-evening streets. 'Like a stranger.' Although he hadn't expected much to happen today, he still felt a strong sense of defeat. Perhaps had he lived as close to the problem for the past few weeks as Keith, he would have seen how situations change only slowly. Keith didn't feel at all the same sense of defeat as Mr Croft. He felt quite optimistic. There simply hadn't been a victory. Not yet.

15

The day of the cup tie was special from the moment Keith opened his eyes. The sun was already casting a diffused glow through the curtains, a welcome change after a week of bad weather, and a warm feeling of well-being tingled through Keith as he sat up in bed. He rested his head against the head-board and listened happily to the Saturday-morning sounds. It was only a little later than the time he woke for school, but Saturday sounded very different from a weekday morning. His father was about for one thing, the dull thud of his hammer in the shed below Keith's window a weekend sound. In the kitchen downstairs the small transistor played children's favourites and somewhere at the back the rhythmic clatter and pause of a lawn-mower drifted along the row. The street at the front was less busy with work-bound cars, sounding more relaxed with the casual clunk of a polished car door, the ring of a dropped spanner.

Cheerfully, encouraged by the evidence of his ears, Keith got up and opened his pink curtains. He looked out over the rows of narrow gardens, the miniature estates of City East. Next door Mr Parsons, tall and untidy in pyjama jacket, braces, and trousers, scraped the black off a piece of toast, and in the garden across the alley a woman with her hair already shampooed and set was hanging out a line full of sparkling washing to shine in the sun. The sky was blue, a bird sang somewhere, and Keith bubbled with excitement. This was the day of the big game. The day City

East were going to beat the league champions off the pitch.

With an explosive cry of 'Come on, you whites!' Keith dropped down the stairs two at a time and went into the back room for his breakfast. He was surprised to see Donovan already sitting up to the table, washed and dressed.

'Hiya, Don,' said Keith, experience telling him not to pause for a reply. 'Poor old Park Lane. In for a thrashing today!'

Donovan's mouth moved in the slight beginning of a smile, a tight-lipped pursed movement, more inward than outward: but a smile nevertheless. Tipping almost as many cornflakes onto the tablecloth as into his bowl, Keith started on his breakfast. As he ate, he kept up an incessant stream of chatter—to himself, to his mother, to Donovan. It was all about the football, but he got no more reaction from the other boy than that first private smile. They were both very much aware, though, of their strong invisible bond.

It was a very happy morning. There was plenty to anticipate. Everyone had high hopes of the day. Donovan keenly wanted to see his old team again, the first feeling of looking forward he had felt since his mother had left. Keith couldn't wait to be swallowed up in the atmosphere of the big match—the crowds, the chanting, the television cameras; while the adults hoped that the noise of the crowd would be swelled in some small way by a sound from the silent boy.

Not far from the deserted Park Lane ground, Mr Croft hurried home from the factory as soon as the hooter went. He washed and changed, but as time was short he decided not to pause to eat. He ran out to his car and started his long battle through the city streets.

As the clock crept round and lunch-time came and

went, his horn sounded off more frequently at the plodding lines of shoppers' cars, the supermarket donkeys, which seemed to be forming into barriers between him and his son. He couldn't afford to be late. He would never find the boy in the packed ground. He had to make it to the house before they left or the boy would think he didn't want him all over again. His was a very special reason for wanting to get through the busy streets quickly. Yet his horn couldn't sound urgent, only bad-tempered like all the rest.

It was a long and frustrating drive. Nobody gave an inch and every traffic light was against him. His left ankle ached with all the clutch work, and when he eventually pulled up outside the Chapmans' house he had a throbbing headache behind his eyes. He only hoped he was in time.

As soon as his car turned into the road, the front door opened and Keith was at the gate. It was all right. He had made it.

Donovan was standing further back in the porch, looking taller than he remembered him from last week even and very smart in flared long trousers and a nylon windcheater.

'Here he is,' Keith yelled back into the dark doorway. 'Donovan, tell Dad he's here . . . '

Donovan turned, but he said nothing. Everyone had thought they could succeed with that catch-him-off-his-guard technique, but it really wasn't that simple. And although this attempt had been unintentional, it still didn't work. There was a silence while Mr Croft locked his car; then Mr and Mrs Chapman appeared at the door.

'I'd make you a cup of tea,' Keith's mother called, 'but the men tell me there isn't time. Have one after. Keith's got a tube of fruit gums each . . . '

'That's all right, Mrs Chapman,' Donovan's father

replied politely. He would have liked a cup of sweet tea with a couple of aspirins, but never mind.

'There'll be a big crowd,' said Mr Chapman. 'We want to get in where the boys will see.'

'Come on then, Dad,' said Keith, two houses down the street already. 'It's ten past two . . . '

Hanging round Keith's neck was the blue and white woollen scarf of City East and in his hand he carried a collapsible fishing-stool which his father had found in the shed. Mr Croft noticed that Donovan was also carrying something—a small square stool of white wood.

'Hallo, boy,' he said. 'How you been this week? OK? You been a good boy for Mrs Chapman?'

Donovan looked up at his father, but his face said nothing. They stared at one another for a few seconds. Mr Croft sighed. He wanted both to kiss his son and to shake him till his teeth rattled.

'What you got there?' he asked.

Donovan made a reply of sorts by holding the stool up higher for his father to see.

'I knocked it up this morning,' explained Mr Chapman. 'In case they can't see . . . when my dad took me to City East in the old days we always needed a stool . . . '

'Very good,' said Mr Croft.

'Good luck,' Mrs Chapman called, ready to return to the washing-up. 'I hope they win.' But before anyone could reply to that, she hurriedly added, 'Both teams.'

The two men laughed indulgently and fell into step behind the purposeful boys, only catching up with them at the busy corner by Fewster's shop. It was then that Mr Croft called Donovan back.

'Here, boy,' he said when his son turned to him. 'I found this in your room: thought you might want it . . . '

Out of his jacket pocket—his familiar weekend

jacket—he produced a neatly folded silk scarf in red, a coat-of-arms at one end and 'Park Lane United' screen-printed along it in white.

'You never go without it at home . . .'

Donovan took it without a word—perhaps not deliberately off-hand, maybe accepting it as a boy does accept something from his father, when words don't seem to be necessary. He wrapped one end round his wrist and let the scarf dangle down the outside of his leg in the current style. Keith saw it and casually did the same with his. Then they all crossed the road and hurried along the thickening pavements to the ground.

City East Football Club had risen to the occasion as if it had never been out of the First Division. A new army of turnstile attendants and programme sellers had been recruited and the Metropolitan Police added their own sense of occasion with their proud and frightening police horses. Peanut men and hot-dog stands had been attracted to the ground like starlings to bread, and souvenir editions of the evening papers had been specially run-off for sale outside the ground. As an all-ticket game it had also attracted its touts, and 'Wanna ticket, guv?' enquiries led to deals of up to five pounds for ninety-pence seats. But Mr Chapman had their tickets, and moving inch by inch to their allotted entrance the Crofts and the Chapmans shuffled into the ground.

Keith had never seen so much smoke. It hung in the air above the pitch in a low, hazy cloud as cigarettes were shared and short friendships were made. Its flat greyness gave added colour to the bright and noisy crowd beneath. Donovan's red scarf was out of place at this end of the ground. The big batch of tickets allocated to the Park Lane supporters were all for the entrances at the far end, away from the home-team's sometimes violent territory, and already down there the swaying red scarves and jumping heads were competing for attention with the chants of the home supporters.

Mr Chapman threaded his small party through the crowd to a spot high up to the left of the home goal where a short stretch of crush barrier still stood exposed. There was room there for the two boys to stand on their stools and lean on the bar, while the men stood behind them. Providing two tall men didn't stand in front it gave a good view of the pitch, and it was well away from the jumping youths who called themselves the City Kop.

Donovan looked at the pitch admiringly. It was lush and green, the white markings standing out against the emerald grass like a highly coloured programme photograph.

'Good surface,' said Mr Croft. 'They can play football today.'

'Perfect conditions for a game,' agreed Mr Chapman.

The two boys leaned on the bar and inhaled the atmosphere, the big occasion, the huge shiver of anticipation which ran over the surface of the crowd. Behind them the men's attention was divided, with eyes for the pitch and ears for the taller of the boys in front. Everything was set. These were surely perfect conditions for Donovan to utter some sound again.

Mr Croft leaned forward to remind Donovan that he was there, that they were together, and he put his left hand on the bar beside his son. With the constant shift of the crowd he would be standing beside him in ten minutes or so, his hand on his shoulder just like the old days.

'Be a great game, boy,' he said, studying his son's face intently. The boy moved his head. It could have been a nod, or it could have been the push they both felt from the squeezing crowd which had filled in quickly behind. He wasn't sure. But a loud boo and a countering cheer made him lift his eyes to see emerging from the tunnel the crisp red and white strips of the visitors, the tanned legs and flowing hair of the Park Lane boys.

'Come on, you reds!' came the individual shouts of encouragement.

'We are the champions!' was the proud communal clap, then the whole sea of rolling red and white joined in the modern song of praise.

'When you walk through a storm . . . '

Donovan looked at Keith, then round at his father. Keith was engrossed in picking out the famous faces as the team warmed up with a dozen assorted balls, but Mr Croft could only see his son.

Their eyes met, at first surprised, then embarrassed, then the flicker of a message passed between them. This is really like old times, it seemed to say. Then Donovan suddenly smiled at his dad. Like his contacts with Keith, it was tight and secret, but as he smiled, his eyes widened in some sort of greeting, and they filled with tears. Mr Croft was too choked to speak. He just squeezed the boy's shoulder hard; hard and tight and possessively. The voices of the crowd swelled to a climax of masculine sound.

'You'll never walk alone . . . '

Two big tears welled up in Mr Croft's sad eyes and threatened to spill over into public view. The colours ran before him, the picture out of focus as the song dipped over the crest to its low emotional end.

'You'll ne-ver walk alone . . . '

Unashamed, Mr Croft let the tears roll freely down his cheeks. Through the blur of his own, Donovan saw them. It was one of those moments: sad, and yet very, very happy.

City East had a lot of fair-weather support. People who hadn't been to see the team for ages had turned out for the big game. So when the home-team ran out to the scratchy sound of 'Blaze Away' they received a huge ovation too:

less organized and melodic, but loud enough to lift the hearts of the selected eleven. More varied in appearance than the Park Lane super-squad, two with balding heads, one very young lad on a schoolboy contract, and a tubby goalkeeper, they warmed up with enthusiasm at the near end, the goal they always chose.

Keith turned round to his dad. 'Turner's playing number eight. And Rodgers is back at number four. Roker's out, he's only substitute . . . '

Knowledgeably they discussed the line-up: the out-of-form player dropped, the teenager brought in. They talked about the back four, the striker and the conventional wingers, and they discussed the best tactics for winning the game. Then a thin, derisive cheer went up as the referee ran out: a familiar figure from television football, Mr Fitzwilliam, short, tubby, bald, his pink knees raised to his waist as he spurted out into the centre circle. Unannounced until the day of the match, this official often gave as much entertainment to the crowd as the two teams.

The captains spun up, and the teams changed ends, City East playing into the goal at the near end. A few photographers stayed there in case the home forwards could put one past Welsh international Chris Young; but the majority of them scurried to the other end like Parisians to the guillotine to see the sharp incisive action of the champions.

All the formalities were over. The referee looked at his watch and waved play away with a shrill whistle.

'Come on, you whites!'

'Park Lane! Park Lane! Park Lane!'

The opening minutes produced dull, safe football. Nobody wanted to be the man to take the chance which let the others through. Keith and his father, all the home supporters, and especially the players in white out on the pitch, knew that Park Lane could turn a benefit match into a massacre. Against a weaker team they would crack in ten if they could; twenty; a hundred. They were drilled to win and win well. They didn't know the meaning of words like 'ease off' or 'charity'. They were a football élite, and they saw their job as not only showing it but rubbing it in. City East, therefore, played a tight defensive pattern, relying on a sudden break from the back to get their forwards going. No chances.

Mr Croft's headache worsened as a feeling of stalemate began to settle over the ground. It was an unconstructive game of stops and starts, the ball continually going into touch from City East under pressure, the referee over-fond of his whistle in his determination to keep control of what could be a bad-tempered game.

The heat went out of the sun as the first of the day's shuttering clouds drifted over the city. The crowd had quietened. They could hear the players shouting instructions about on the pitch. Nobody else was making any noise. Mr Croft rocked backwards and forward on his heels impatiently. The chances of the crowd getting excited enough to prompt Donovan to make any sound of support seemed to be getting more and more remote. This wasn't how Mr Croft had envisaged things going at all.

Mr Chapman seemed to read his thoughts.

'Needs a goal to cheer it up,' he said.

'Yes,' said Mr Croft, his headache beginning to take on the intense pain of a migraine. Beside him, Donovan was still and silent: engrossed in the game but not communicating any excitement. He couldn't. For the crowds on the terraces it was a very dull first half.

It seemed very different to the players out on the pitch. Every ball had to be chased for and won. Every forward on the field had to be marked as close as the fit of a second skin. Every man had to use so much sheer effort in concentrating that the concentration itself became a physical drain on energy. And when the whistle went for half-time, the players felt they had played a full match already.

Mr Croft found just enough room to sit down during the interval. The pain was pounding with the pulse behind his eyes now, and he sat and rubbed them with the backs of his hands, like a bear with a bee-sting. He felt sick, and he badly wanted a cup of sweet tea and some pain-killers. At home he had special strong tablets for this sort of thing, but he didn't carry them with him. Usually he would just hurry home from work, take a tablet, and put his head under the bed-covers until the pain passed. Now, trapped in the crowd, there was nothing he could do. They would have aspirins in the bars or at a tea-counter, but he knew he wouldn't get near one without queueing through most of the second half. And he was determined not to leave Donovan's side. That was where he belonged. He had to be with him, talking to him, sharing the game with him, just like old times. He pulled himself up as the teams walked out for the second half.

'Good game to win, boy,' he said to Donovan.

Donovan had been thinking about the game during the interval, while he was listening to Keith. He could see how difficult it was to penetrate a packed defence, even with superior skill. He agreed with his father. Once more he nodded. It was such a simple action, taken so much for granted by most, but it had an electrifying effect on Mr Croft.

His eyes widened with surprise. There was no doubt about it. Donovan had really nodded. The headache faded for a moment. He grew excited.

'A goal will do it,' he said. 'Just one goal.'

He could have been talking about the winning of the match. Mr Chapman knew otherwise.

'Yes,' he said, 'I think you're right . . .'

The whistle for the re-start took their attention back to the stalemate on the pitch. In a game as tense and tight as this they knew that someone had to make a mistake some time. And when the first slip was made early in the second half, it was made by Park Lane. Mr Croft knew it was a stupid unprofessional error for which they might well expect to be chewed up by their manager later.

The City East goalkeeper cleared a long ball down the middle, a high, hopeful ball which could go to anyone, which the old pro's called 'picking up the pieces'. The opposing centre-half would go for it, he would probably win it and head it forward again, while a second wave of the attack ran in ready to snap up the loose ball and get something going. On this occasion it worked. Langton, the City East goalkeeper, used his area well and kicked the ball way up above the level of the stands to drop like a stone deep in the Park Lane half. Peter Wall, the England centre-half, big and strong with a long streak of cunning, judged it well and got his head to it: but Mr Fitzwilliam failed to see Pond, the City East number nine, hold his shirt and tilt the international off balance. As a result the ball bounced off the top of his head and landed luckily at the feet of Brooks on the City East left wing. Park Lane, playing a tight offside game, were standing square as the slight winger touched it forward to Arthur Morris.

'Offside!' shouted half the ground.

The cry was repeated by four red-shirted players, who stopped immediately and raised their arms in the air, their heads turning as one to the nearer linesman. But to their surprise he held his flag firmly down.

'Play on!' shouted the referee, loudly enough for everyone in the ground to hear it, and he waved his arms and high-stepped at speed after the attacking Morris.

The roar was deafening. The goal was a formality. Even

in the Third Division one man can usually beat a goalie left on his own. As Chris Young dived bravely for his feet, Morris scooped the ball up and lobbed it well over the goalkeeper's head to bounce innocently into the net like a baby's beach-ball.

The crowd went mad.

'Offside, ref!'

'Goal!'

'Where's your glasses, referee?'

'Goal!'

'The referee's a bottler! The referee's a bottler!'

'Goal!'

'Offside!'

'Easy! Easy! Easy!'

Nearly everyone had something to shout, a yell for, a cry against. Keith threw his arms in the air and let out one long shout of triumph. Mr Chapman threw back his head and shouted too. Faces scarlet, eyes wide, mouths locked open, throats sore, the City East supporters yelled their delight at the white shirts who were hugging and dancing before them like washing in the wind.

When the goal was confirmed and the ball was kicked back to the centre circle, Donovan and the Park Lane supporters had every reason for being silent. The First Division giants had fallen heavily into their own offside trap, and like novices they had stopped to appeal instead of trying to retrieve the situation.

Mr Croft summed it up for Donovan.

'Silly goal,' he said. 'That's a cup-tie goal, boy, real silly.'

Donovan's mouth turned down slightly in glum agreement.

'We got to go out and play now,' his father said, 'all the pressure is on us . . .'

He kept looking at Donovan, hoping for a word in

agreement, but the boy said nothing. Keith could see the disappointment on Donovan's face.

'Bad luck for your side, Don,' he said in a hoarse voice. 'Cheer up, it's only a game.'

Donovan moved his mouth in a small, sad smile. You can say that when you're winning. He looked at Keith, who, if anything, seemed more worried than he was now that his own team was ahead. Donovan had the strong impression that Keith might even have preferred the goal to have gone the other way for some reason.

For the rest of the second half the Park Lane attack tried everything it knew to beat the tightly packed City East defence. A white shirt hardly ever ventured into the opposing half of the pitch. The whole team fell back and marked and double-marked the Park Lane strikers.

Watches on forty-thousand wrists were consulted regularly as the game went on in the same square pattern of play and the end of the ninety minutes drew dangerously close. The hands on Mr Croft's work-scarred watch were hard to see through his painful squinting eyes; but he knew how things stood. With the onus on the opposition to score, the City East boys only had to keep the ball out now. Every shot was beaten away by a boot, a body, or a head. Long clearances into the crowd, time-consuming and to the whites' advantage, were greeted with loud cheers and countering boos. Time was rapidly running out. But it couldn't go fast enough and the continual professional pressure of the Park Lane players eventually brought an advantage.

Toki Balabaka, a young Nigerian-born left-half in his first season with City East, had defended with great skill and commitment throughout the game. In partnership with left-back Everton Lloyd they had held off the darting runs of Henderson and Prentice with courage and a good understanding. They could do no wrong—until Balabaka brought Henderson down on the edge of the penalty area. As the red forward came at him with the ball, Balabaka slide-tackled him with a sideways scything movement, missed the ball, and took the man's legs from under him. The foul looked worse than it was, and Henderson played it up by diving as far as he could into the penalty box. 'Penalty! Penalty!' Mr Fitzwilliam had seen the location clearly, however, and he refused to listen to the Park Lane appeals for a penalty. But he was just as determined that the offender should be booked.

'It wasn't that bad,' Mr Chapman commented.

'Never a foul at all,' said Keith.

There was a wait while Mr Fitzwilliam put Balabaka's name in his notebook, a wait which the crowd used to good vocal effect, rising to a crescendo of roaring noise as Taylor elected to take the kick.

'Off! Off! Off! Off!'

Any free kick taken by Jimmy Taylor, the Park Lane captain, had somebody's name written on the ball. His accuracy with a dead ball was legendary, and Park Lane was noted for its skill with set-piece scoring chances. This plan was simple. Taylor would loft the ball to the far post on to the head of big Peter Wall. Wall would head it back across the goal mouth, and from there it only needed a touch from any one of four forwards, or an unfortunate defender, to put it in the net. Cunningly, Wall didn't advertise the plan by standing at the far post to be picked up and marked. He hovered way outside the box, nearer the corner flag, ready for a swift and accurately timed run-in.

Donovan knew the plan. So did Mr Croft. They had both seen it used often before up at Park Lane. Its success rate was high. And if it ever needed to succeed it was now. There wouldn't be much time after this. Mr Croft forced his head up through the pain of his migraine to watch the kick.

'Wall!' he said to Donovan. 'It's for Wall. Watch that Wall.'

Donovan nodded again. Unbelievably, in the mingled pain and tension of the moment, the nod was taken for granted.

Mr Chapman looked at his watch. 'It's nearly time, Keith,' he announced. 'If we can survive this we've made it!'

The tension began to tell all round the ground. The crowd went suddenly silent as the ball was placed in position, re-positioned, and finally turned round by Taylor in a nervous gesture. In the long silence he backed away from the ball, counting his steps.

Wall stood ready to begin his run in, clear of any close defender: and the whole Park Lane forward line strained to go when the ball was released.

Mr Croft's arm tightened round Donovan's shoulder and he leaned his head close to his son's, pretending to see through a gap. This could be the moment he had waited for. He prayed that it would be.

For a moment no one seemed to breathe. Taylor ran up to the ball, and with a loud plunk he kicked it up into the air in a graceful arch towards the far goalpost. Wall had begun his run with Taylor, and as the ball fell, supposedly a goalkeeper's ball—and loudly claimed as such by the City East goalie—he leapt past three men and met it with his head. Catching the entire City East defence off balance, the ball shot back across the goal and Henderson's head met it first time: a perfect execution.

The waving bank of red at the far end was already shouting 'Goal!' when the ball struck the bar and fell back into play at Henderson's feet.

For a second he didn't know what to do. He had already

half-turned to celebrate his goal when the ball came back to him, and his bewilderment was obvious throughout the ground.

'Shoot!' yelled the Park Lane crowd, hands beside heads, faint eyes covered.

'Shoot, man!' shouted Mr Croft in Donovan's ear. 'Shoot!'

He took a quick look at the boy. Donovan was leaning over on the bar, on tiptoe on the stool. His arms were held out in exhortation. His eyes were blazing. His mouth was open. With the rest of Park Lane he was willing, commanding, the flustered Henderson to shoot. He *had* to shoot. But he could say nothing. He was like a bronze soldier on a war memorial silently shouting the charge. And when Everton Lloyd cleared the ball from Henderson's bemused feet, he sank back with the rest of Park Lane, in silence.

One giant voice groaned its disappointment over City East. Mr Croft's head pounded as he squeezed his son again. Never mind, boy, he seemed to say. Don't worry, it will come. Then he removed his arm and pawed his eyes again.

When the final whistle blew, Keith didn't join in the loud shout of City East triumph. Neither did Mr Chapman. There hadn't really been a victory at all. They had both been aware of Donovan's failure, and they both felt as bad about it as Mr Croft.

'Don't worry, Don,' said Keith, taking his turn to embrace the sad boy. 'You can't win 'em all. And you did win the league . . . ' he added in consolation.

The crowd at the near end buzzed with excited talk as the two teams trooped off the pitch. A fight broke out on the Park Lane terraces. The loudspeakers thanked everyone for coming and the canned music played.

Suddenly Mr Croft departed.

'I've got to go,' he called to Mr Chapman. 'I've got to get a tablet at the tea-counter. I'll see you outside . . . over the road . . .'

Then he made off into the crowd. As he sidled through the slow and contented streams of supporters his head dropped lower and lower. His Adam's apple felt a hundred times too big. The disappointment hurt inside: and his head felt as if someone were trying to pull his eyes out by the roots. He must have a tablet. The pain was intense. The migraine was almost as bad as the night of the quarrel. Then it had been bad like this all day. He had come home from work in great pain that night and he had put his head under the covers. How could anyone act reasonable with a pain like this? Now he wished he had never come up.

Never.

16

Keith's father led the boys out of the ground through the scattered peanut shells and the gathering piles of paper. Although they waited a full five minutes before moving, the exits were still bottlenecks when they got there, and Keith and Donovan had to link arms so as not to lose one another. There was a buzz of excited sound. Most of the crowd around them were talking about the unexpected win. None of them had really given City East much chance. A few radios held above the bobbing heads gave out the news of other cup ties, and when the knowledge of who else was through began to spread amongst the crowd, they started to speculate about the draw for the next round.

'Arsenal's through. A penalty. How about Arsenal?'

'Or Leeds. I'd like to see Leeds down here . . . '

Keith didn't feel much like talking. There wasn't much he could say which wouldn't sound like crowing to poor old Donovan. It took the edge off it really, seeing him so disappointed.

Mr Chapman went before them, his tall figure a landmark for the boys. He heard the comments of the people around him; on the face of it he had every reason to be as happy as they; but underneath he was thinking about Mr Croft. He was sorry for Mr Croft. The man was clearly cut-up about the boy not saying anything that afternoon. At one stage he had obviously thought the boy would, and at the end, when everyone was shouting 'Shoot!', Mr Croft had been on the top line for Donovan to say it too. But

189

when he hadn't, the look on Mr Croft's face had been unforgettable. Like a father at the birth of a still-born baby. On the other hand, the more Mr Chapman thought about it, the more he realized that no one had promised that Donovan would speak today. It had only ever been a chance. They'd all thought the circumstances were right, and they'd all worked themselves up thinking it was bound to happen, when it hadn't been bound to happen at all. Things don't work just because we want them to, he thought, and it was silly to be disappointed when they didn't.

He edged his way past a hot-dog stand, the warm smell of the fried onions making him feel hungry. He supposed they'd better ask Mr Croft back to tea. It was the least they could do.

A few metres behind Mr Chapman, Donovan followed the blue and white scarf which was back round Keith's neck. His eyes concentrated on the bobbles of knitted wool, the blue wisps hanging off, the light and shade in the white squares. He drew in a deep sad breath. During the last week, since the trouble with Fluff and Keith's kindness, he had begun to see more of what was around him. He had begun to feel more as if he was part of what was going on, as if he mattered again. He felt important to someone. That terrible hurt in the pit of his stomach wasn't there all the time now. It only came and went. It came when he thought about his mother, when he saw her face, felt her hands, smelt her soft sweet smell; it came then and he was cut-up inside with longing. But it went as well. It didn't come quite so often, and it went. It went when he did things with Keith, when Keith wanted him to be around, when Keith talked to him and said good things. Then Donovan began to feel alive again, a part of the world.

He had begun to emerge into the outside again like a

patient from a hospital: he had begun to make a recovery, but for a while he would be convalescent.

Part of that pain had gone. But now he felt a different pain: the pervading hurt of failure. He had been with his father, Keith had been there, he had seen his Park Lane team play. He had felt good: warm, content, and happy, as if the nightmare had ended and he had woken up to find the sun in all the dark corners. He had had a pleasurable feeling of belonging where he was. It was just like the old days. Then, in the game, Henderson had dithered with the ball—he did that sometimes—and everyone else had shouted 'Shoot!' at the tops of their voices. Donovan had wanted to shout 'Shoot!' with the rest, pleased to do so. He had opened his mouth and shouted. Or he had thought he shouted. But in fact he had only shouted as in a dream, the harder he had tried, the further he had slipped from success, and the words ringing clearly in his head had been only silence to the others.

Donovan knew his failure well. It had a poisonous taste. For the first time for weeks he had wanted to communicate, and the sound he needed to do it with had refused to come.

Head down on his chest again, he followed Keith out through the big gates. They crossed the road in a wave of people, the cars forced to halt like woodlice caught in a stream of ants. Mr Chapman led them into the doorway of a closed shop, and there they waited for the crowd to thin, Keith and his father on their toes looking for Mr Croft.

It must have been ten minutes before any of them saw him. In his search for tea and tablets he had had to go deep into the hollow grandstand to a general-purposes bar where a large crowd of celebrating men were making the most of the afternoon licence. He queued for a long time, but he got what he had gone for at long last, and when he came out again he made straight for the nearest exit from the ground. It turned out to be fifty metres or so further down the road than the gate the others had used.

Mr Chapman saw him first, looking this way and that, puzzled at the roadside. The crowd had thinned by now, but there were enough people standing about to bewilder Mr Croft momentarily.

'There he is,' said Mr Chapman. 'Down there on the other side . . . '

'Hey! Mr Croft!' shouted Keith. But he was too far away from the man to be heard.

Mr Croft looked about him, seeming to get more and more agitated. Then he made to walk further down the road to the next gate. He had completely lost his bearings. Instead of going towards the group he was seeking, he was about to walk off in the opposite direction.

'Run and get him, Keith,' said Mr Chapman, 'or we'll lose him and we'll be here all night . . . '

Immediately, Keith darted out after Mr Croft. He ran straight into the road which had just recently been a pedestrian thoroughfare, his eyes fixed on the disappearing Mr Croft.

The car bearing down on him was first seen by Donovan, before Mr Chapman even. It was coming fast down the one-way street on the near side, the driver laughing with the man beside him, his attention lost in the enjoyment of a joke. Donovan saw it all like a flash photograph—with Keith in the foreground in the path of the car.

Without a second's conscious thought, Donovan yelled:

'Keith! Car! Look out!'

Keith heard the cry and turned instinctively back to the safety of the pavement. Hearing the roar of an engine, he threw himself forward, tripping over the kerb, and with a nasty hard crack to the head he landed on the flat slab.

The car driver, jerked back to his senses by the fright of almost running down the boy, hooted his horn in anger and drove on his way with a curse. But he eased his foot off the throttle. He had missed the boy by no more than a few centimetres.

Keith's father picked him up, lifting him under the armpits and dragging him into the shop doorway like the victim of an urban explosion. The boy looked stunned. His face was deathly white and his eyes rolled. Mr Chapman took away the scarf from around his neck and tried to sit him up. Keith rubbed his head where it hurt. Gradually, a hazy idea of where he was came back to him. He was in the street, on the pavement, leaning up against a wall. His dad was there, and some other people. A lot of them were talking, but amongst the blurred colours and the muzzy voices he felt sure he could hear the heaving sobbing wail of a boy crying, a throaty full-blooded cry which seemed almost to take pleasure in the sound it created.

In all the noise Keith could hear a familiar voice, a man's, very close, soft and gentle, talking in a calm and comforting way. Was it speaking to him, or to someone else? He couldn't quite be sure. But he seemed to be saying something . . . something like . . .

'There, boy, let it out. Let it all come out. Cry all you like. For your daddy. Everything's going to be all right. Just you see. All right. Just you see . . . just you see, boy . . .'

Then Keith lost consciousness again, and he floated off into the darkness for a while. The next thing he knew he was being piggy-backed along Transport Avenue by his father, with Mr Croft propping him up at the back and Donovan holding on to a dangling hand. He looked down at the other boy and smiled. Donovan smiled back. It had all seemed like a dream.

'All right, Don?' he said, weakly.

Donovan nodded. They walked on a few more paces.

'Yes,' he said. 'Yes, Keith . . .'

17

Mr Roper walked through the busy playground, wishing he had worn his vest. It was Monday and the first chill morning of autumn had come without warning. Some of the children, caught out too, shivered in a cluster by the cellar steps. And Teddy, who was always there with the cleaners, looked faintly blue as he stood in his shirt, shorts, and plastic sandals on his own by the school door. A little later than usual, Mr Roper took a straight course through the games and dared a ball to hit him. He hadn't gone far when he was surrounded by a small group of younger children.

'Sir, sir . . . '

'You know that kid . . . '

'Please, sir, guess what . . . ?'

Another dramatic tale to tell, Mr Roper thought. He groaned inwardly and prepared to listen to them. The first hints of bad news always came from unlikely sources. Often wrong in detail, they were usually right in spirit.

'You know that boy who can't talk, sir . . . '

Mr Roper groaned again. Oh no, he thought, don't say someone else has hit him or something . . .

'Yes?'

'Well, please, sir, he can, sir.'

'He can what?'

'Talk, sir. Over by the lavvies, sir. He swore!'

'Swore?'

'Yes, sir . . . ' They warmed to their task. 'Please, sir, he told David Smith to get stuffed!'

Mr Roper's surprise was sparked by more than just the words the boy had used. If this was true it was indeed a breakthrough.

'Oh well, that's good news,' said Mr Roper. 'Very good news . . . whatever he said . . .'

'Will he get into trouble, sir?'

'I doubt it,' said the headmaster. 'No, I doubt it.'

He broke away from them and ran up the steps into the school, while the little group turned back, their duty done.

'We told him,' they said to anyone who would listen. 'We told him.'

While the dinner-monies were being collected, Mr Roper sent for Keith. It was now some time since the early unhappy days when Keith had been up outside the headmaster's door. This time he felt both happy and confident. Mrs Cheff came along from her office and talked with Keith for a minute or so before she went into the head's room.

'Hallo, Keith,' she said with a smile. 'How's everything?'

'All right, thanks,' Keith replied. 'Very good,' he added, smiling.

'Mum and Dad all right?'

'Yes thanks.'

'And Donovan? How's he?' She hadn't heard the good news.

'Great,' said Keith with another big grin. 'He can talk now. He started Saturday, after the football match.'

'Really?' questioned Mrs Cheff, the surprise showing dramatically on her face. 'Oh, that is good to hear. I'm very, very pleased.'

'Yes.'

Still murmuring her pleasure, Mrs Cheff tapped on the crinkly glass of the door and entered the room. Did Mr

Roper know? she wondered. She liked to be the first with news.

But Mr Roper did know, and within a few minutes he was getting the whole story first-hand from Keith—the disappointment at the football, Keith's narrow escape from being run down, and Donovan's warning cry.

'Well, I think it says a lot for you, lad,' Mr Roper commented at the end. 'He obviously trusted you, and cared for you, and you see, it worked wonders.'

'He saved my life!' Keith said. 'He's my mate, my *brother*, an' he saved my life.' And it didn't seem a strange thing to say.

A theme for assembly was forming in Mr Roper's mind.

'But tell me, how has he behaved since Saturday? Has he been talking during the rest of the weekend?'

'Yes, sir,' said Keith, 'bit by bit. Not much to start with, but he said "please" and "thank you" and he asked for another glass of milk; things like that . . . '

'Well, I'm really delighted, Keith,' Mr Roper concluded, getting up and putting his straggling hair back in place. 'I'll come and see him in a while.'

When Keith returned to the class there was something of a festival atmosphere in the room. It was like Christmas, or the last day of term. There was general laughter and chatter, and people were out of their desks.

It had all started when Donovan had spoken, and now Mr Henry was acting as if a baby of his own had said 'Da-da' for the first time. It had only been a thank you for an exercise-book returned, but it had been clearly audible in the silent classroom, and Mr Henry had gone as far as he could to declare a public holiday. Everyone could move about for ten minutes, he had said, and talk to one another about what they had done at the weekend. 'Instead of writing it in your diaries,' he had explained.

Dave and Tony were standing over Donovan. They were having a giggle about something, and Donovan was smiling tolerantly. Keith joined them.

'What's up?' he asked, suspiciously.

'It's all right, Kee,' said Dave. 'I just told Don I only wanted to hear him talk this morning—when I kidded him I wanted a fight . . . and I'm not a flipping turkey to get stuffed . . .'

Keith was pleased to smile too. He would have to be a bit careful with Dave, he wouldn't trust him too far. If Dave thought you'd stand up to him he'd offer to be your friend. All the same, it was good to be talking to him again. And Tony.

'See you at playtime,' said Dave. 'We'll pick up for football.'

'Yes, see you,' replied Keith. He didn't answer for Donovan. He left him to do it himself.

'OK,' he said. 'If you like . . .'

It was still strange for Donovan to hear his own voice again, coming out sounding like someone else's. It seemed a funny voice to him, like when he'd first heard it on a tape recorder; but no one else seemed to notice. Everyone, all day, just seemed to like to hear him talk.

When the boys got home from school a surprise awaited Keith. Mr Croft was there, taking a well-earned but unaccustomed afternoon off.

'Here, Keith,' he said. 'This is for you.'

He gave Keith a small brown-paper parcel—a small square package which felt heavy and looked very interesting, the sort of present he opened first at Christmas.

Mr Croft looked more relaxed today as he stood by the table, smiling, while Keith tore off the paper. Keith looked up at Donovan, but the boy gave nothing away with his face. Keith opened the small cardboard box which was

198

inside and revealed a smooth pad of tissue paper which lay protectively across something special underneath. Gently, he lifted it off. What he saw brought a broad grin of pleasure to his face. Taste! Sitting there like models in a showroom, shining with newness, were two miniature electric racing-cars, an Italian red and a British green. They were perfectly proportioned and beautifully finished, the sort collectors buy and never race.

'They're great,' said Keith, jumping up, then adding inadequately, 'They're just what I wanted . . . '

He shook Mr Croft warmly by the hand. Mr Croft smiled.

'It's the very least I can do, boy, after what you done for me—and Mrs Croft . . . '

'But how did you know?' asked Keith with a frown. 'How did you know I needed some new ones?'

He looked at the smiling faces in the room. His mother's, Mr Croft's, Donovan's . . .

'I told him yesterday,' said Donovan. 'I remembered, Keith, and I told him . . . '

ABOUT BERNARD ASHLEY

The Trouble with Donovan Croft was one of the earliest books to set a school story in the state system. Nineteen other gritty novels have followed, as well as over forty shorter books — including picture books, and 'junior' stories like *Dinner Ladies Don't Count*. He has been shortlisted for the Carnegie Medal three times, and won the 'Other' Award with *Donovan Croft*.

Bernard trained to teach at Trent Park College, specializing in Drama, following this with an Advanced Diploma in Education at the Cambridge Institute. He has been headteacher of three primary schools, two of them in London, before retiring from teaching to devote himself to writing full time. He has also written for television and the stage, his serial *Dodgem* (from his own novel) winning a Royal Television Society Award for the best children's entertainment of its year. His play, *The Secret of Theodore Brown*, played at London's Unicorn Theatre, and his stage adaptation of his own novel, *Little Soldier*, is published for performance by schools.

Bernard lives in south London and is married to Iris Ashley, herself a former headteacher, and has three sons, two of whom are headteachers (Chris Ashley also writes children's books), and four grandchildren. He has been honoured in recent years with Honorary Doctorates in Education (University of Greenwich) and in Letters (University of Leicester).